Chanchal Sanyal is an entrepreneur in the live events and activation space of the advertising industry, currently based in Gurgaon. He has been at various times—sometimes concurrently—college lecturer, itinerant traveller, advertising professional, business owner and now, writer.

A resident of Delhi, he has seen the city grow, evolve, mutate and spawn a Noida and a Gurgaon in hastily contracted marriages with its neighbouring states. The city and its peoples are of endless fascination to him.

The Glass House

*A Year of
Our Days*

Chanchal Sanyal

RUPA

Published by
Rupa Publications India Pvt. Ltd 2018
7/16, Ansari Road, Daryaganj
New Delhi 110002

Sales Centres:
Allahabad Bengaluru Chennai
Hyderabad Jaipur Kathmandu
Kolkata Mumbai

ISBN: 978-81-291-5165-0

First impression 2018

10 9 8 7 6 5 4 3 2 1

The moral right of the author has been asserted.

Printed at Repro Knowledgecast Limited, Thane

Dedicated to the millions who have invested their millions to living in our cities.

Day 1

𝒯HE LAPTOP BATTERY is at 91 per cent. The time is 9.01 a.m. All the signs are right. All the lights are green. Just go ahead and do the deed. Take that decision. Sign the agreement. 9 lakhs and 10 thousand rupees need to be paid now. That's all. After that, it's all construction-linked instalments. In any case, that'll either come out of the salary or a housing loan can be taken. It'll be easy...and at least the EMIs would be for your own home and not to thicken the wallet of FatBum Khanna.

'So, have we come to a decision, dear partner and provider? Are we on the brink of realizing our middle-class dreams? Moving into our own home and climbing one step higher in the Maslowian ladder? In addition to roti and *kapda*, will we finally have a *makaan* now too? Or will our time in the NCR be clocked by the Khanna monthlies forever?'

Ten years of marriage and Roshni is still as slim, as head-turning gorgeous, as the day I first saw her. Her tongue too is as sharp; if anything, it has become sharper. I know that each of her statements is a question, and I also know that she doesn't really want an answer because she has wandered off to reprimand Sitarabai for not dusting the bookshelf. Good that she did not wait for my response; even better that I did not open my mouth to offer any pearls of wisdom regarding the virtues of renunciation and non-attachment versus the Maslowian security of property ownership. I can imagine those shapely eyebrows rising, the left one first as always, and that particular tone of voice, like water being poured over ice cubes, 'Really Embee?! This is not your classroom, you know. And all we are doing is buying a house so, what is the need for all this philosophy, pray?'

But at least, my dear wife of a decade-plus has left behind a cup of fragrant Lipton tea and two Marie Light biscuits for me.

It's a bright Delhi end-of-January morning...or as bright as Delhi mornings now get. The sun is bravely battling the fumes of the millions of vehicles that rampage up and down the city's roads every day and its light is reflecting off the glossy real estate brochures I am studying. Propped up on two pillows, I am the lord and master of my rented two-bedroom second-floor flat and like the Emperor Alexander, I am surveying what frontiers I can conquer next. Rosewood, Greenacres, Richmond, Fairydale, Glenmont—all smile at me from brightly coloured and expensively printed brochures. All these are of course located in the middle of Haryanvi villages which means that beyond the walls of Richmond are the slums of Rasoolpur and the view from Fairydale Views is actually of Fazilpur's fields.

Wow! This can certainly be a business school branding case study—Fairydale in Fazilpur! But, once again, I am evading the main issue. It is decision time and Roshni has narrowed it down to two prospects. My only call is financial and of course getting the geometry and the geography right which basically means I need to ensure that the living room and our bedroom should be in the same line and get the sun in winter and the shade in summer. These are the simple diktats of my simply better half.

The builders are more or less the same in terms of reputation and work. The specifications offered are again six of one and a half dozen of the other—laminated wooden floors, vitrified tiles, dado, ceramic finish, etc. All the reviews on the Internet uniformly promise the most grandiose returns on investment. In fact, come to think of it, the top hits are so alike that it seems they've hired the same social marketing firm. The sample flat illustrations of both look right out of the pages of the best interior decoration magazines. The pricing is the same as are the terms of the CLIPS (Construction Linked Instalment Payment Scheme). The excel sheet that is open on the laptop is powerless to choose from and Roshni has, in her wisdom, left the choice to me—so she can blame me later, no doubt. Too many decisions for me, a simple college lecturer—sorry, Associate Professor—to take. Time to go downstairs, stretch my legs and take a smoke break.

'Arre, *humare Bungali saab.*'

Too late to duck behind the unfolded newspaper, and sidle right back up the staircase to my second-floor eyrie. I am ambushed, fair-and-square, at the ground floor entrance by the kurta-pyjama-sweater-and-dressing-gown wearing apparition of FatBum Khanna.

'Please come, please come, Bungali saab. Come and have some tea and mithai. Arre, I know you can't say no to mithai. After all, you are Bungali, *na*! My boy is having some problems with his Class XII Political Science syllabus, please come and help him.'

I know from past experience that any expostulations of my being a lecturer of History would be in vain. So, I smile, fold my hands and follow him in meek surrender. FatBum Khanna is not just a person; he is a force of nature and is as imperious and decimating of all in his path as the most unstoppable ocean tsunami. The very idea of a thin, prematurely balding, bespectacled, cigarette-smoking Bengali academic countering him is simply ludicrous. Why did I ever step out for that cigarette? No wonder, it's proven to be dangerous to health.

Mr Khanna is a second-generation Delhiite. His father was a refugee from what is now Pakistan, and was the original owner of the plot of land on which Mr Khanna built the house, the second floor of which I rent. This is not his only house. Khanna & Khanna ('Arre, my boy will join me in due course, of course!') are well-known realtors of this area and own a string of properties including small hotels and smaller offices. Khanna saab is a well-respected and slightly-feared local businessman whose hotels frequently rent out rooms by the hour to people of great influence. I am often told, and I also know, that I am lucky to have him as my landlord. Our domestic nickname for him, 'FatBum', is not just a reflection of the imposing size and impressive acreage of his posterior, it is more accurately a reflection of our own insecurity and jealousy. Perhaps it is the inverted snobbery of the intellectual for the materially successful. I know that he is fond of me and is proud of the fact that his physically-closest tenants are an intellectual Bengali and his designer wife. He has let this be known on occasions and his 'fondness' for us has caused susurrations of 'lucky' to ripple across our social fabric. Whether that 'lucky' has been satiric, ironic or wistful, it has depended on the occasion. For example, at an evening soiree with the Danish ambassador where Mr Khanna too is invited as he happens to be one of the biggest dealers of a Danish manufacturer's goods, the 'lucky' that escapes from the botoxed lips of the PR lady definitely sounds sarcastic; but, when our next door neighbour Mrs Sachdeva sees us never having any problems with the local municipal authority, the same 'lucky' sounds wistful. We live in that interesting time of a society's evolution where luck is contextual.

'Uncle, you are dreaming again and I gotta go. I am telling you, this is just not worth it. Dad's not completely with it yet, but you know what I mean? I'll get the papers—the question papers you know—before the exams. The boards are gonna be a breeze. We know this guy who takes only 5 lakhs per paper. Don't worry, it's all set,' says the other Khanna of Khanna & Khanna, Vishal ('call me Rocky'). With his father's height but none of his bulk, the youngster's physique is chiselled like a blade, thanks to daily sessions at the gym. And, no doubt the entrepreneurial spirit and business acumen that can visualize the innovative 'out of the box' way to get good marks in the board exam, and make the capital necessary for the venture available, are inherited from a long line of Khannas.

'Didn't sit, no? I knew it. Must be doing some jugaad. *Baap ka hi beta hai, sala!*' With this expression of paternal pride which leaves me deeply confused, Khanna saab also affirms that he keeps as watchful an eye on his personal matters as he does on his business goings-on. He knows. And he lets it be known that he knows.

'So, Bungali saab,' he says, folding his hands across his ample stomach and settling heavily into a padded chair. Khanna is now looking at me as a scientist might look at a new species of microbe under the microscope. Obviously his ambushing me at the staircase was no accident and has a deeper purpose than asking a mere neighbourly favour.

'What is this I hear? My hospitality is not good enough? Now, you want to be a landlord too?' Mr Khanna knows of our home-owning ambitions. And he is letting it be known that he knows.

If there's anything that my reading of history has taught me, it is this—to win battles, make allies and co-opt to a common cause. The tumultuous history of the subcontinent resonates with this from the time of the Mahabharata right until the alliances of perfidious Albion and let us not even get into the politics of the present day. So, why not use it one more time?

To employ Rocky's favourite utterance, 'Right here, Right now.' Now was the time for an alliance between the Bengali Brahmin and the pushy Punjabi.

'Arre, Khanna saab! I was coming to you to discuss. The fact is that I need your help.' My opening salvo hits home. FatBum does a double take and settles deeper into his chair. Any supplication made to him whispers to the long-buried strains of imagined royalty in his DNA and fairly shouts to the lawgiver and arbitrator of those with less fortunate fates— something that he sees himself as nowadays. This is the man who has seen the movie *Sarkar* four times and I am sure the track, 'Govinda, Govinda', has started playing in his head. Appropriately enough, his communication becomes regal and non-verbal. An uncrossing of the arms, the upturning of the right palm and the slight flick of the wrist…all these urge, well, actually, grant me the permission to speak. I have the ear of the God-with-the-Big-Ass.

'I cannot seem to come to a decision. I am confused, maybe because I do not know enough about the subject. I think that you are the best person to discuss this with. Like everybody, Roshni and I have a dream of owning our own home; you know, to sit in the balcony and have a cup of tea in the morning knowing that this is our own property. Please don't misunderstand. We just want a place, you know, our own home. A man should have it, don't you think? Perhaps, you could help us understand how this builder game works. I am so very confused.'

Yes, I am babbling and sounding incoherent even to myself, but I seem to have, somehow, hit the right notes. Khanna is connecting the dots. And wonder of wonders, he seems to be turning sentimental! He is lumbering out of the chair and advancing towards me to shake my hand. Taken unawares, I can only manage to offer my hand and cannot even get up in time to meet his advance. He grabs my one hand with both of his and proceeds to surprise me further,

'Bungali saab, I always thought that you were those scholar intellectual types, you know, how they are…completely dry! But now, I see that you are emotional, just like me. Yes, yes, of course a man should have his own home, otherwise, how can he be called a man, *na*? This is my grandfather's lesson. He came here with nothing but the clothes on his back. First thing he did was to build his own home. A house is a very important thing—it is a symbol you know, a mark of who you are. Of course, I will help you. I will clear all your confusions and maybe, I'll help you with money and all. But, first, Bungali saab, you must know how important a home really is and since you are a scholar, you must read this. It is a book that my father also read, and I have read it too. It is very important to understand what one's own property means. It has been written by an Indian fellow only, that's why it is so relatable.'

With this, FatBum bends over the cracking laminate of his drawing room showcase, pulls out a dog-eared paperback, blows the dust off it, and ceremoniously hands it over to me. With complete disbelief, I note that I am holding in my hands a tattered copy of the 1981 Penguin edition of V.S. Naipaul's *A House for Mr Biswas*.

Day 22

$\mathcal{T}$HE UNSTOPPABLE ELEMENTAL force that Mr Khanna unleashed has swatted away every obstacle in our path to home ownership. Agents of both the developers have been called to his office. One has been made to wait while the other is being grilled; and both have been told that negotiations are active with the other. Best rates and best discounts have been mercilessly extracted and now the conversation has moved into the arcane realm of cash and cheque, of black and white. Representatives of no less than three banks have been peremptorily summoned for disbursing loans. Our combined financial papers have been dressed up to be made almost unrecognizable to us; it seems that the easiest way to get a loan, and to get it on the best terms, is to seem to be in the least need of it. Our investments, along with heirloom purchases and gifts of stocks and shares, have been collected, collated, dematerialized and what not. It seems that we are not really as badly off as I thought we were. While all this has been happening, I have, on most occasions, been a mere mute spectator. Nothing in either my education or experience has prepared me for this and Khanna saab in full flow is a tough act to follow, even for those who are schooled in this sort of thing. Increasingly, the staffroom has become my refuge but even there, unlike the previous experiences of my life, I am loath to share what is happening. Not because I am fearful of arousing the jealousy of my colleagues—the jealousies and insecurities of small-time academics in small-time colleges like ours can be fearful monsters—but because I am feeling a strange kind of unmanning. It is as if in the act of having my own property, of imprinting my place in the world; in this act of making my mark, in this ultimate expression of maleness, I have surrendered my right to Khanna.

'You know, he doesn't even steal a look at my tits when he's talking to me nowadays,' says the better half.

'You mean to say he used to before?!'

'Of course. He's even tried to cop a feel too, once or twice. That's okay. Every Indian male over the age of 14 does it and every Indian female over the same age gets used to it. It's when they don't or when they stop doing it that you know something is wrong.'

Roshni, now between 33 and 34, is at the age that for some women is the full ripeness of womanhood. Always an attractive slender-waisted, big-bosomed head-turner, it seems that the same nature that has denied her motherhood has instead focused its energies on making her even more attractive. As she pronounces her observations on the symptoms of Mr Khanna's malaise, she straightens up over the flower-bed container she has been watering and the heads of the flowering Phlox gently caress the same breasts that have lately been so sadly bereft of the benevolence of Khanna's attentions.

'Now you're staring. Well at least, there's nothing wrong with you! Sometimes, I think that this home-buying thing is not working out so well for you. You really haven't been yourself these past few weeks. But, hang on, let's complete this topic, this FatBum Khanna thing, what's going on? Has he adopted us or what? Very fatherly he's become, coming up to the second floor every day with advice-shadvice and whatnot. And this

Mrs Khanna?! That's another story! I mean, even when she was collecting her monthlies this time, she asked me, "Beta, are you sure?" Sure of what, I ask you? What charms have you been working on her MB, you old thing?'

We are on the extended terrace of our second-floor two-bedroom flat. Actually, it is the terrace of the third and fourth bedrooms of the first floor that have remained unbuilt on this floor. Roshni has appropriated this space for her container garden and now it runs riot with flowers and vegetables of every hue and colour. Once again, nature compensates—whatever Roshni touches seems to burst forth with compelling vigorous life. Her paintings, her garden, the fashion designs for which she is justly famous, everything pulsates with a lusty vitality; everything, but her own womb.

'Well, it's just that Khanna saab seems to have taken it upon himself to ensure that we get our own house in double-quick time. He—'

'And pray, why would he do that? I am sure there's some ulterior motive, he's just not the type to do something for nothing. He will definitely want you to swing college admissions or something for that brain-dead son of his.'

Roshni is, as always, probably right. There will be a sting in this tale. Khanna will spring some 'obligation' on me in due course. I know as well as the next man that no favours are ever dispensed for free. However, for now I am content to let the seductive appeal of home ownership, the promised bucolic magic of Glenmont Greens—yes, that is the development we have chosen—insulate me from the realities of life. I know that there will come a time when one will have to awake from these roseate dreams, but then, I tell myself, that time is not now.

Now is the time to watch my wondrously endowed wife carefully weigh a large circular, glisteningly purple brinjal in her hands, deciding whether or not it is ripe for plucking. The plant is in an earthen pot mounted atop an iron stand so that one does not have to bend while tending to it. Roshni, holding the brinjal and assessing its weight while gently bobbing it up and down on its stalk, is wonderfully backlit by the setting sun that renders the top that she is wearing practically transparent. Once again, I marvel at the sure instinct of the female of the species. To be so artlessly artful—at most times seemingly so unaware of the effects that she creates—and yet to be so much in control of the situation, almost as if it were an orchestra and she, the conductor.

'Arre uncle, always thinking-shinking! How about some doing-shoing? Papa wants to see you downstairs, everything is approved. Your loan has come through and the buyer's agreement is ready. Please just go down and sign. Open a bottle-shottle, time to celebrate, *na*? It's only a matter of months that you are our guest here. And aunty, here, let me help you with that.'

Another player has been summoned up to the orchestra. Rocky is here. Bounding up the stairs wearing his track bottoms and black thermal sleeveless vest, pumped up and perspiring, he is obviously back from the gym and is full of excitement with the good news he brings.

Bravo the English language! Bravo for the way it can be slapped around by anyone to mean exactly what they want. This is a language that will forever outlive the wet little people of the wet little island that gave it its wet little birth. A language that is so wildly accumulative, so intensely fertile, so endlessly accommodative! What else could have so effortlessly conjoined bottle with *shottle*? Thinking with *shinking*? Doing with *shoing*? No doubt, these cognate pairs will become standard for the language, as English as chutney, camera, pyjama and bungalow.

And that's where, historically, Sanskrit failed us. After all, it was 'Samskrit' or 'complete' or 'fully finished' to use a Rocky phrase and, therefore unable to accommodate anything new.

These were the thoughts that were banging around my head as I clattered down the stairs to meet FatBum Khanna. And, then I stopped...the Rocky phrase. Rocky. Rocky, the six-feet-two-inches muscular hunk who sent me downstairs is no longer the pimply Khanna Junior of two years ago. While I am ruminating, literally like the cud-chewing cow, on the historical muscularity of the English language, somebody else has been gaining a literal muscularity. Has my blindness for Glenmont Greens blinded me to other goings-on too? Or is it just that my masculinity is so insecure that it suspects a 'two-birds-with-one-stone' has just been pulled? Uncle is downstairs and aunty is upstairs with Rocky, manually assessing the weight of gently bobbing objects.

Day 43

'MR B IS the mover. Ask him, after all, he is the one moving to Gurgaon. Perhaps he'll change jobs too, become a corporate animal and all, you know, not have to bother with the likes of us anymore.'

Malati Patel is the resident bitch of the staffroom. I guess every staffroom or every office has to have one. Sleek as an otter, with her beauty parlour-washed hip-length hair that is today a shimmering waterfall (or should that be a hairfall?) over her designer hopsack top and her shapely Hugo Boss denim-covered bottom, every word that drops from her Maybellined lips is pure poison. And today, I am the unfortunate target. I often wonder why this should be so. No, not why I should be the target, but, why a person who has everything that everyone else desires should be so bitter about it all. Malati and her businessman husband live in their own home in an upscale South Delhi colony and have everything that money can buy, foreign holidays included. For her, this job is a hobby and certainly not a requirement. It is something that helps her dust off the covers of all the books that she had read as an English Lit post-graduate student at Miranda House many years ago. She has no economic compulsions and no health issues. She is the daytime version of every student's English Lit teacher wet dream and yet, a profound unhappiness resides at the very core of her being. Perhaps, this is the truth of the human condition that just material things and good looks alone do not make us happy; perhaps, for some, making another unhappy is the only thing that creates happiness. Or maybe even happiness is overrated? Why should anyone crave it? Malati certainly does not seem to.

'Oh ho! Not even bothering to answer, are we? Have we already moved to the Gurgaon condominium set, hmm? Club membership done? Corporate appointment letter in hand already?'

'No no…Malatiji, nothing like that. These things are not for people like us. I was actually thinking about the loan amount and how best to reduce it. The bank has given us a three-month window to do it without prepayment penalties.'

'Well, I hope you are not asking me for a loan now, are you? My husband may seem rich, but you know how these things are.'

This unasked-for disclosure of a patently false financial status coupled with an exaggerated about-turn leaves me staring once more at a definitely stare-worthy Hugo Boss clad derrière. Maybe this is what, without the contribution of Mr Boss, serves to console Mr Patel and compensates for what passes as Malati's conversation. Have I at last stumbled upon the secret of marital togetherness—not a priori but a posteriori?

'But why in the world are you taking a loan? It is really beyond me. I heard from my husband's bank that you have just reactivated your demat account and even got a trading account opened. So, you must be big into the share market, *na*? Why would a person like you need loans? In fact, I think all of us should take investment tips from you on how to make a killing in the market. That's really what I heard and that too from the bank.'

'What big ears you have Malatiji and what big mouths the

people at your bank seem to have. The account was reactivated only because it became dormant; there was no activity for the last six years. And the trading account was added because it is needed to sell shares which is what I am doing, selling every last one of them to pay for the house. Does that qualify me to become your investment adviser? Feel free to try me out.'

Pin-drop silence. Necks stiffen perceptibly all around. Had human external ears been flexible, a lot of them would have swivelled around to this new rat-a-tat action. The impolite Bansal actually cranes forward, abandons the pretence of correcting answer sheets and turns his chair to face us. Poison lips meet the suddenly machine gun repartee Bengali. This is too good to miss in this starved-for-entertainment staffroom.

I said it, but I don't believe I said it. Forever the shy and introverted academic, here I am blasting off with both barrels. And finishing off with a double entendre too—an invitation no less.

'Mmmm… Maybe there is a Vesuvius under the sensible spectacles. Maybe I will Mr B, maybe I will, indeed.' And then, once again, it is the Hugo Boss winking away as Malati leaves in a whiff of Chanel.

'Taking a chance with Princess Patel? You are certainly more adventurous than you look, my dear Dada. Has she given you her phone number yet? There is a process to these things. Now, the WhatsApps will start, that's the way to go. But believe me Dada, don't commit things on text. Be general and vague. Make the commitments and fix the times and the places only on phone. That's the right way to do it. No footprints Dada, no evidence.'

There are some people who automatically make you look at the seat when they get up from it. They make you look at the ground as they walk on it. They make you look for the trail of slime, the oily malodorous residue that their presence must leave behind.

'What are you looking behind for, Dada? Look forward. Look ahead. This is a new beginning. You are making your first house, maybe you will also have your first affair, huh! Dada, my advice is to get another phone—one for business, one for bizzzinesss—heh heh.'

Not dignifying this human slimeball of a colleague with either a reply or a name, I manage a grimace in his direction, fish out the car keys from my pocket and leave the staffroom at a brisk pace. I have had enough education from this temple of learning for a day. It is time to leave behind the assorted fauna of this academic zoo and decide with Roshni the date of what the builder has called the 'site visit'.

February is turning to March. This used to be the perfect season in the Delhi of my college and growing-up years. A clear crisp cold that made you want to swing your arms in the shade and laze around with your eyes closed in the sun. There used to be wide empty roads that one could jog down in the mornings, breathing lungfuls of fresh air and careen drunkenly up on borrowed motorcycles after a night of partying at college hostels. Traffic roundabouts that used to burst into orgies of psychedelic colours at this time of the year complete with proud gardeners—or the humble *sarkari maalis*—crouched in the hedges waging mortal combat with every last defiant weed. This was the Delhi where the *chaiwallah* would offer you a free chai when India won a test match. The Delhi where people from all over the country came to see the roads and marvel at the speeds of the cars.

All that has long since disappeared. The air is now soupy, not as much inhaled as sipped. The traffic does not flow... it ebbs back and forth, as if to prepare itself for a final push that will take it hissing and panting till the next signal, where this convulsive, almost peristaltic behaviour will be repeated. This is now the Delhi where I am stuck between a DTC bus and PB license plate wearing, 'Proud to be Punjabi' bumper-stickered Toyota Fortuner SUV which seems to be pederastically inclined towards my tiny Alto. I turn the music a notch up and desperately try not to catch the eyes of the fiercely bewhiskered and turbaned Fortuner driver in my rear-view mirror. For some reason, in addition to being bewhiskered and turbaned, he is also maniacally grinning.

Keep calm. Don't catch his eyes. Think pleasant thoughts.

This is the holy trinity I keep repeating to myself. And then completely unbidden, the image of an un-Bossed behind comes to my mind. After all, what did she mean by that 'Maybe I will Mr B, maybe I will indeed'? And, wasn't there a 'Mmm' before that? And a little more of the swing in that Bossed behind afterwards?

Does the buying of a house function like a dose of mental Viagra? I am imagining an avatar of myself that is completely the polar opposite of the reality. Imagine, a woman like Malati Patel actually 'trying' me someday!

'*Jaago mohan pyare. Jaago!*' The Fortuner sardarji is at my car door and the bus in front of me has moved. Since I have not, the traffic behind me hasn't either. No wonder the sardarji is screaming. Once again, while I have been dreaming, the world has moved on and I am quite literally in the same place. Mouthing hasty apologies to the irate sardarji who must be wondering as to why this fellow is waiting at a traffic signal and muttering continuously into his cell phone, I engage the gears and move forward.

Much as I hate its traffic, much as I hate its rudeness, much as I find it impossible to breathe its air, there is still something about Delhi. At least, there is something about it for me as an individual. Maybe it's the oft-repeated cliché of the everlasting fidelity of the 'first love'. I came here as a callow teenager, fresh out of school, to study History at Kirori Mal College and promptly fell in love. This, after all, is the city of the seven cities and is, in fact, the only place in the world where all the historical cities live together at the same moment in time. This is the city where a twenty-first-century slum shares a wall with a sixteenth-century nobleman's mansion. The city where migrants from Rajasthan use the stones of a seventeenth-century mausoleum to build their makeshift huts. The city where Manoj and Geeta of Sarojini Nagar inscribe the date of the third-month anniversary of their everlasting romance on the tombs of conquerors who laid claim to half a subcontinent and whose edifices and gardens the world has marvelled at for 500 years. Delhi for me is the ageless wanton beauty, confident of her charms and careless about the ceaseless fascination she exercises. Not for her, the sanitized security of 'protected monument', the alienation of 'historically significant building—do not enter'. Not for her, the prissy concerns with hygiene, environment and plain good manners, and certainly not when they get in the way of living the most out of this life. This city has so much that she simply could not care less if everybody has a go at her. There is always enough to go around. Hasn't it been that way for centuries? After all, what could the twenty-first-century man do that millennia of marauders could not? Add in a few more millions of vehicles? Or tens of millions of more people? Block the river with sewage? Choke the skies with filth? Build flyovers when the roads were not enough? Add in the metro and the monorail when the flyovers needed to be flown over or burrowed under? 'Bring it on!' this city seems to say, 'Is that all you got? I've seen worse. Bring it on and I'll still show you how to have a good time baby.'

Just as I am about to record the climax of my urban love story, the cell phone beeps with a strident urgency. It is, as foreseen by that staffroom slime-ball, a WhatsApp message.

'Sorry. Did not mean to offend you. Congrats on the house. All the best. Can we make up over a coffee in the staffroom? Malati.'

Princess Patel has spoken. I have to look at the message twice. The 'staffroom' clinches it. It is actually Malati Patel. Of course, I did not have her number stored in my phone. She is apologizing...to me? And, asking for a coffee...with me? Suddenly, the traffic in front of me clears up. The road is once again a delight to drive on.

Day 64

IT'S BEEN TWO months since the games began. Every time I think I have learnt the rules and the moves, something changes. Every week I think I am becoming better at it and every weekend I learn something that shows me how bad a player I really am. This is becoming a distressing pattern…from the shares I sold at what I thought were a great price to the 'top-up' home loan I got at what I thought was a great rate. In both cases, FatBum Khanna made his displeasure, actually disappointment more than displeasure, clear. 'Professor Dada, you should really leave these things to me; you see how those shares are climbing now, see, you only see. And you did know about my sister's nephew's brother-in-law. He works in the same bank, at the Janak Puri branch. Obviously, he would have gotten you a much better rate. Why go through an agent? And if you really wanted a top-up, you should have asked me, na? After all, am I not the same Khanna who organized your home loan in the first place?'

Obviously my landlord was batting in a different ballpark and had a perspective that was completely different from mine. Much more galling than this sort of frank remonstrance at my attempts to play the game without the coach was what I heard a week ago when I was climbing up the stairs to my second-floor flat.

It was late in the evening and I had gone out for a smoke.

Coming back, I noticed that the Khanna's ground floor living room door was half-open and sounds of jollity were spilling out into the night air. This is the door that connects the ground floor with the outside staircase and I had to willy-nilly pass it on the way up. With one foot on the bottom step, I was debating whether to go in and say 'Hello' or walk straight up to my flat. While wrestling with the relative politeness and convenience of either option, I heard something that had me transfixed like a rabbit caught in a torchlight. Simply, it was the sound of my own name. Such is the human psyche that the sound of one's own name always resonates sharp and clear, cutting through all the babble and ambient noise. Above the clinking of glasses and sounds of Punjabified English, the mention of 'Bungali Dada' was like a siren to me. What made me inch further towards the open door and steal a look inside was the helpless laughter that followed the mention of 'Bungali Dada'.

It was the typical Khanna evening 'get-together'. Two generations ago, this would have been held on cots made from jute ropes, placed under a tree with water from the well, *matthis* from the *chulha* and home brew in clay cups. Now, of course, it was in a posh South Delhi living room with the menu catered to by 'Colonels Kababz' and with Scotland's contribution to world civilization graciously lubricating the conversation in cut glass and crystal. However, the people had not changed as much as the environment. I could make out four couples, three of whom I had met earlier, all close friends of the Khannas and all similarly successful business people. 'Gurgaon flat, *haanji*. Can't leave him alone for one minute, *naaji*. Don't know what he will do next. Can't negotiate na. No sense of the real world. Reads lots of books, but, not enough chequebooks, *haanji*!' Gales of laughter follow this witticism. FatBum is holding court and there is a riveted audience for the risible antics of the bumbling

Bungali. To me, this cuts deeply. There is genuine affection from Khanna. I can make that out and I am sensitive to it, but what galls me is that I have become a party 'item', the evening joke, something for FatBum to dine-out on.

How do I explain to this well-meaning yokel how much I enjoyed the interaction with the home loan agent? Abhijeet Prasad and I have so much in common. Both of us came to Delhi after Class XII and both stayed back in this city to make whatever we could of our lives. He went on to become, in his own words and said with a quiet pride, a 'home loan professional', and I moved on to the groves of academia. He and I spent four afternoons together, with him taking me through all the intricacies of interest loading, prepayment penalties, floating rates versus fixed rates and everything else. For all this, if nothing else, the 1 per cent extra on the top-up was well worth it. Obviously, I cannot explain this to FatBum and I am not even going to attempt any explanations because they would be wasted on one for whom 'sensitivity' means allergic reactions ('*Haanji*, my Patialawali sister's *devar*, you know brother-in-law? He is also sensitive to sulpha drugs.'). And, as for shares, they were mine and I sold them when I thought right. I may not be a champion of this game but I am a trier and I will stick it out right until the bitter end, no matter how much I am laughed at and certainly no matter by whom.

But why this belated bitterness, this sudden stridency? That incident is a week old already. There has been time and more to toss it aside, to expunge it from the mind and to move ahead. So, why now?

Today is the day when we go for another 'site visit' to see how much of our dream has become a reality. There seems to be an almost festive feel to the day. Roshni has been in a bright cheerful mood since morning and I have benefitted. Fresh orange juice, aaloo paranthas with butter on top, mango pickle and curd. All this on a day when according to the schedule, it was my turn to make breakfast. Like most couples nowadays, we divide the list of to-dos in the house and when one is suddenly released from the morning duty, it is all the more welcome for being unexpected. Plus of course, the quality of the food is an instant mood elevator. On my best days, I can whip up a mean butter toast with eggs to order—omelets with chopped chillies, onion and coriander, eggs sunny side-up or over-easy, scrambled or boiled—all these are part of my repertoire, but it stops there. Boiling potatoes, mashing them, making paranthas out of them—this requires a level of patience and skill that is much beyond me. Roshni has actually been singing while making breakfast, something that I am tempted to join her in. A song from *Gharonda*—'Do Deewane Iss Shahar Mein'—is the song of her choice. This song used to be a favourite of ours during our early days of courtship and marriage when we would joke about setting up a home together. Now, when the setting-up of the home is actually happening, Roshni is singing the same song. Obviously, all is right with the world.

'There, just carry this basket out, will you? There are cucumber and tomato sandwiches, a grilled paneer and pistachio salad, actually a mixed nuts salad, and all sorts of fruits. Here, don't forget the drinks; there's freshly squeezed juice in this one and a protein shake in this one. I'll just take a quick shower, change and be there. Hope you are ready?'

A packed picnic basket! Roshni had made much more than just breakfast; she is obviously treating this 'site visit' thing like a day-out, a picnic. And indeed, why not? It is after all a big day for us. It is the day for seeing the progress of our dreams, the realization of our hopes. It is the day when we shall literally see the concrete symbol of our togetherness take physical shape.

However, I can't help feeling that after a breakfast of aaloo parantha, pickles and curd, this sort of health food basket seems a bit strange. No matter, she must be trying to balance our diet. Wasn't it just the other day that she was talking about 'we are what we eat' and hasn't her latest fad been health food? She must be trying to get me to cross over to the 'healthy' side of the tracks.

'Ready? Shall we go?' Roshni is all set and I can't help but do a double take. It's been quite some time since I've seen her take such pains with her appearance and the results are, frankly, spectacular. Her dense, tightly-packed curls are peeking from under a sun hat. Perched atop her pointed nose are designer sunglasses that accentuate, rather than hide, the lovely oval that is her face which is, in turn, touched over with the faintest traces of makeup. She is wearing a fitted white top that leaves her arms bare and caresses her curves while inviting strategic attention with embroidered frills to the cut that is halfway down the front. The ensemble is completed with a belted-on blue skirt that comes to just below her knees. The overall effect is disconcertingly schoolgirlish, rather a very mature and knowing kind of schoolgirl look. Before I could comment on what she's looking like and how it's taking me back to ten years ago, Roshni hustles me out of the house and casually mentions over her shoulders as she locks the front door, 'Oh! Did I tell you that we are going in the Khanna's Innova? Mr Khanna wanted to have a look at the site and Rocky is driving us.'

It is true what they say about black clouds sliding over the sunniest of days. The day just went dark for me, like a bulb being turned off. My worst suspicions burst like a nuclear bomb and the fallout turned everything sterile and grey.

The chirpiness, the girlish excitement, the health food provision, the desperate dressing-up to turn back the clock...

all this was for the six-foot-two hunk—Rocky. You were just the convenient cover. The second 'deewana' of the song is not you, you deluded middle-aged fool, it is the ripped drinker of the protein shakes. Didn't you figure it out? You supposedly smart man, your drink is the Lipton with the extra sugar, not as if she does not know it. What? Lost your smarts too, have you? And since when has she started showing off those lovely arms and legs for you? Actually, more to the point, remember when she stopped showing those to you? C'mon, be honest, man up! At least, here, man up. Do you remember the last time the two of you had sex? Balding, middle-aged butt of all jokes, off to build a house are you? Realize your dreams? Create that cozy nest? You might want to check out the cuckoos flying in and out of that nest first, you blind old fool.

Rocky is in the driver's seat. He is wearing a baseball cap with an intertwined NYC logo embroidered on the brim pulled low over his curls; a sleeveless hoodie displaying those bowling-ball shoulders to their best advantage, blue jeans and white Nike trainers. This is what FatBum, with perspiring paternal pride, calls his 'Hrithik Roshan' look. Roshni too is sitting in the front. They are consulting a map and occasionally their hat brims touch, their bare shoulders too. There is a casual intimacy about them that is completely excluding FatBum and me sitting at the back. At least, I think so. Honestly, I feel isolated, alone and miserable. In a surreal sort of daydream, I imagine myself picking up a spanner and banging Rocky over the head with it, screaming all the time, 'I've heard about it. I've seen those films too. I know all about your fascinations with MILFs. She's not the one for you. Leave her alone. Alone! Alone! She's not even an M, how could she be your MILF?' Equally surreal, I see the sequel to this as well. Rocky calmly disarms me of the spanner, reaches behind and pats my skinny left knee with his large and heavy right hand. 'That's perfectly alright uncle, perfectly alright. I'm perfectly OK with WILFs too.'

'Arre Professor saab, what is wrong with you today? Why are you so quiet and withdrawn? After all, we are going to see your very own flat today. If anybody should be unhappy, it should be me. I am losing you, *na*? Arre, today is a big day for you. It's your first own flat. It's your *nishana*, your *ashiana*. C'mon, c'mon, be happy.' Khanna's elephantine as well as infantile attempts to cheer me up have penetrated to Roshni. She leans behind and speaks, 'Khanna saab, just leave him alone. He is a tremendously moody person. He will snap out of it in his own time. Or maybe, he won't. Our saying or doing anything will not help. He builds up worlds in his head and finds his own way out of them. Here, you please have a sandwich. Embee, here's one for you too.'

Have I really? Have I really, Roshni, my dear? Have I really built up this world in my own head? That's what I keep thinking while mechanically chewing the sandwich. In all fairness, I can't also help noticing that Roshni is hardly behaving like an adulteress now, or at least, she is not behaving like a person with a guilty conscience or one with anything to hide. She is perfectly free, completely unselfconscious and keeping up a running banter with both the Khannas. So what? Am I building this in my own head? Or is it that Roshni actually has no guilt on her conscience about what she is doing? That is, if she is actually doing what I think she is doing. Does her guilelessness also mean guiltlessness? Or is it that I am just going plain batshit crazy? The funny thing is that I have never suspected Roshni of anything like this ever earlier and now suddenly this has burst upon me with a full-blown certainty. There, she just patted Rocky on the shoulder to show him a signboard, and I almost leapt out of my seat to physically force them apart.

'Here we are uncle. Here we are. This is the main Sector Road that leads up to Glenmont Greens. Won't be long now. We should be able to see the site in ten minutes.' This communication from Rocky forces me to snap out of my thoughts and look around. Here we are? Where are we? This looks like some sort of desolate moonscape. A road that has been ravaged by earthmovers on either side and scarred in the middle by some bulldozer run amok...this is 'here we are'? The Innova is lurching from side to side, splashing through pools of rancid water and Rocky too is muttering about the damage to his beloved car. On either side are glass and concrete buildings adorned with the names and logos of the world's best-known companies and in-between them, like cavities in teeth, are empty plots or half-constructed shells of buildings. There are people, smartly dressed in office formals and carrying laptops bags, who, for some reason, are rushing across the road. There seems to be an urgency and purposeful efficiency about this place that, for me at least, does not correspond with the physical reality. It all feels a little disembodied, one psychotropic remove from the 'here and now'. Like a play where the actors are merely rehearsing and all the props have not yet been put in place, but somehow, someone has collected the ticket money, let the audience in and raised the curtains. Just what is this? And just where are we?

Roshni too seems a little shocked. 'Khanna saab, the last time we came here, this was a proper road and there were lots of trees on either side. I remember two-way traffic with a paved central verge. There were light poles and trees on the central verge too. Just what happened here?'

'Progress happened here, beta, progress. And, sometimes, this is the price of progress. But, why worry? It's for the better and is only temporary. The fact is that the builders have now got this converted to a Sector Road, so the government is now putting in drains on either side, that's why all this is happening, you know, progress.'

'But the central verge?' Roshni's incredulity is apparent and in spite of all my problems, I cannot help but be interested in the conversation. This urban planning lunacy seems to be, in orders of magnitude, higher than the craziness in my head.

'Beta, that is for the Rapid Metro. You know, Gurgaon needs to be serviced by its own mass rapid transit system. It is, after all, a smart city, a twenty-first-century city. So, this is progress.'

Wow! So, that's what it is. Silly, deluded me. I thought it was a case of the urban planners mistakenly interpreting the urban planning manual in reverse... Or perhaps perpetrating a horrible practical joke on the gullible public. In fact, I can even imagine them huddled around a conference room table with the projector displaying the 'Action Points' of the final meeting.

'First we do the horticulture, you know, plant all the trees. One must first think of the environment, na? Then, we build the buildings. Let them out on rent or sell them. Revenue is important. Then, we worry about the roads. After all, all those buildings will have all those people and they will need to move to and fro. See, we always think about the convenience of the people. So, now we build the roads and the roads...oops! Those roads will have cars which will need to stay tethered to the buildings... No matter, we let the people park on the roads for now. Oh ho! What a nuisance, those people will have bodily movements, you know. They will eat, shit, etc. and will need water, electricity and suchlike. Okay, so next, we dig up the roads and lay in the sewer pipes, the water connections, etc. By now, the rush of people will be too much, the roads will be clogged with cars with no parking space, so let's now build a rapid metro. See, this is the modern thing to do; it's happening all over the world. Of course, we will build it on top of the existing roads or atop whatever by now passes for a road.'

All action points discussed, the meeting is just about coming to a close and I can just imagine some bright-spark Babu—perhaps the senior-most of them all—maybe one of the exalted IAS, rapping the table and pronouncing, 'I have a value addition to maximize efficiency, reduce downtime and rationalize costs.' Of course, everybody is now waiting, faces aglow with excitement, fingers poised over laptops to minute these words of divine wisdom and transform them into an 'order'. 'Let us,' says he, 'do it all together. We will build the drainage system and the metro rail together. That way we will maximize efficiency and rationalize costs. Of course, after that we can worry about the horticulture and the parking issues. That's later. We need something to do tomorrow too; after all, nation-building is a continuous process. But let's be efficient and offer the best developmental strategy and execution to the public.'

'Let's do it together boys,' he says and voila! Here we are... sloshing through yet another pothole—and wow—here's a herd of goats! Here we are with the roads dug up on both sides, and not to miss, also the middle. After all, this is 'maximized' and 'rationalized' progress.

Imagined scenarios aside, the fact is that with the astounding clarity of thought and purity of intelligence that these people are known for, the civic planners invested in plantation and horticulture 10 years ago. Three months ago groves of fragrant neem and flowering mayflower trees over tens of miles were uprooted to lay in the roads. While the tar macadam was drying on these shining ribbons of progress, the civic planners were once again struck by a bolt of inspired vision—sewers! Or perhaps they were working to the agenda. So, they have now dug up all the roads to lay in the sewer pipes. No doubt, displaying the same brilliance of sequential logic, they will arrive at telephone lines, fibre optic cabling and electric wiring too. Till then, we gaze open-mouthed and unbelieving, pinching ourselves to wake up, reminding ourselves of the epochal moment at which we stand in history—this is a civic dream unfolding, a vision becoming real, the first Indian city of the millennium is taking shape before our own eyes. What's more? As a shining example of originality of thought and stout independence of spirit, we have declined to copy examples from around the world. Hell! America made her cities a hundred years ago, we will make our own, in our own way. We are the children of the millennium and this is our way and if it is different from what our ancestors did four thousand years ago in Harappa and Mohenjo-Daro, so be it. Yes, even today, those sites are held up to the world as examples of superb town planning, but wait…it took four thousand years for that to happen. No doubt, four millennia later, Glenmont Greens and its environs will be the new poster boys of livable, breathable, walkable cities.

FatBum is nattering on and on to Roshni about the 'politician builder nexus', 'driven by investors not end users', 'difficulties of land acquisition', etc. It is a boring and needlessly defensive monologue… I know all this. In spite of all evidence to the contrary, this academic is not exactly an ingénue in these matters, but, right now he could not care less. He has dismissed this as the madness of the metropolis. Right now, he is thinking of getting back at Roshni. How dare she do this to him? Was this what she learnt at her 'Hindi-Medium School' at Meerut? Is this why he is building a home with her? So, what should he do now? Have another coffee with Malati? Yes, he's already had one as a peace offering from Princess Patel. So, what now? Another one? How pathetic is that? A coffee? No, two coffees.

Maybe even three. And is that enough payback for what the wife is doing with Rocky?

'Will you snap out of it or will I have to make you?' Roshni is shaking my shoulders and hissing at me. The car has stopped and I can make out she is very perturbed. The schoolgirl-look is coming apart; there are sweat stains on the pristine white of the top under the armpits, the hair is in disarray and for the first time I am seeing her in a Virago mode. Well, in all fairness, I have never seen her in an adulteress mode either. Shaken out of my stirring thoughts, I see that Rocky is helping her out of the car. One foot in the car, one foot across the puddle in which he has perhaps deliberately parked, and with the wide-open stance of Hercules, he actually swings Roshni out of the car on to dry land. While I have been dreaming about coffee, some things are happening right in front of my eyes. I don't want to see this anymore. I want us to go back.

We are at the entrance of a massive gate that has 'Glenmont Greens' etched over it. Beyond this, there is nothing but a cavernous pit. It seems to be terraced and there are earthmoving machines crawling out from inside it. It is obviously the foundation for the building.

'Let's go back. If the only mark of our effort at homebuilding is a hole in the ground, I am not interested yet. Let's go back.'

The ride back is a silent and sombre affair. For a day that started so well, this is especially anticlimactic. Obviously, no one understands the reason for my moods and by the end of it, nobody is much interested either. Mr Khanna thinks I am some sort of manic ingrate or actually, he is just puzzled. A person with his uncomplicated and simplistic zest for life just cannot comprehend why someone should not be jumping with joy at seeing the foundations of his dream being laid. How can I tell him that for me that dream is turning sour? If, as is obvious, these town planners are certifiably insane, then who would be madder than me to invest my life-savings here? If I am to build a nest, do I have to install a watchdog for the cuckoos? Thinking all these thoughts and watching my dreams mutate into some sort of horrible diurnal nightmare, I watch Roshni get off at her Zumba class while Rocky drives us home. I do not say bye. She does not look back. This uneasy silence I know will not prevail. This is merely the calm before the storm. Before the day is out, there will be words. Many words. Loud words... between Roshni and myself. I know it, I want it, and I dread it.

Day 85

I LOVE THIS place. There is something warm and homely about it. Something that is so practical. Something special for every kind of person who comes in. Ask any ten people about Aitbaar and you will get ten different opinions. And mark my words, not one of them will be negative, all will be complimentary. That is the beauty of this bar. It is different things to different people, different people know it differently and yet it is a common favourite.

Maybe that's what I am missing out in my understanding of Roshni? Maybe different people know her differently and like her differently and maybe her understanding of them or understanding with them is different. After all, I cannot be expected to understand all the understandings.

I hate that evening. I will always hate it. There is so much ugliness under every relationship. What could bring that ugliness to the surface and could make it bare its frightening, repulsive, malformed face for all to see…this will always remain an enduring mystery for every couple. That evening was all ugliness.

A tall and statuesque mountain with green grassy slopes and fat white sheep cropping the sides, flowers blooming in every valley and dale, rivulets of the purest water running down as babbling brooks… That could be the picture of every relationship. And then one fine day, maybe for no fine reason at all, the volcano erupts. Tongues of flame and clouds of poisonous gases shoot miles high into the skies. Molten, burning lava pours down the sides, torching everything in its path. All that beauty is reduced to a smouldering ruin reeking of poisonous fumes. After that, where does one even begin to rebuild? Where and how does the first flower bloom? Or the first green blade of grass appear?

There was so much shouting that night. Roshni and I have had fights earlier (which couple doesn't?) but this was not like a fight. This was more like a war to death. Inflict the maximum wounds with no thought of injury to the self. This was not a quarrel between two friends; it was as if ten years and more of hidden grievances, slights and insults were just looking for a vent to explode and those ten years came out in two volcanic hours...this was mortal combat between sworn enemies.

Wonder if we will ever be friends again? Friends like that, like that green grass covered hillside. And what is this? I *smell* grass. Is somebody smoking up? Definitely smells like grass. Oh! I am on the Aitbaar balcony now. There are many people around, smoking. Like I said, it's a warm friendly place. Homely. Unlike home now. Think I'll have myself another whisky...with water please, soda gives me acidity.

Why did I have to confront her? Not only that, confront her with no evidence? Nada. Zilch. Nothing, but the product of my fevered imagination. I put 2 and 2 together and came up with 22. The doggy posture. And then, why did she have to react like that? She is the one who normally laughs at my imaginings and dismisses them with her trademark long drawn-out, 'Emmmbeeeee, come down to Earth boy, you're flying again'. How come she flew off like that? Started screeching, 'How dare you?!' Answer me that, I ask you. Why did she overreact so much? Answer me that. There must be a guilty conscience somewhere.

And how dare I what? All I asked was for her to settle my

misgivings? Is that too much to ask, I ask you? After ten years of marriage, I ask you. So, why bring in all that 'after all I do for you? Stay back in Delhi when I could be in Paris, London, New York—anywhere?' So, did I ask you not to go? And where does my 'lack of masculine security' come in? How dare you…is that not hitting below the belt? Why the senseless crudity of 'just because you are not having sex these days, you think I'm fucking any Tom, Dick and Harry?' First, I am not having sex because you are not having sex. Second, it was neither Tom nor Harry, it was Rocky. Specifically, Rocky. Dick, we'll allow generically.

One more whisky please.

I miss the green grass. Really, I do. I even miss those stupidly bucolic white sheep. I guess our thing will never be the same thing again. Wonder if it'll ever be a thing again at all. Why did I ever have to open my big mouth and bring in my Psychology 1.0 into it? It was really after my pompous 'you are treating this house thing like the baby you cannot have, so, you are preening up and sending out the wrong signals' that things went really south. Why did I ever have to say such stupid shit? Doesn't it sound like shit? Shit that's deliberately and provocatively, coldly and calculatedly designed to hurt? Am I really that guy? And is she really the shrieking banshee who, after that, went, really went, after my mother, my father, my lack of professional achievement, my lack of ambition, my being an absolute unmanly loser and everything else.

Three weeks since. No rapprochement. No signed armistice. No entente cordiale. Maybe an armed truce with occasional border skirmishes. Roshni and I are nowadays merely bristling at each other. Three weeks have sapped us of the energy to jump at each other's throats and tear our eyes out. We are sleeping apart and conversation is limited to the necessities. Now, rather more than less, I hear the sniffles from the bedroom in the guest room where I currently sleep. Myself? I am tired, really tired. Like I said, I miss the flower-strewn hillside. I miss it terribly. I wonder if flowers bloom on cooled lava?

I wonder if one more whisky would be just right?

Amazing! While it sharpens the mind, it blunts the tongue. That's what that one more whisky does. The mind is crystal clear. It is seeing things as they are. It is also noticing the waiters exchanging looks and sniggers at the thin balding guy smoking on the balcony whose tongue is unfortunately blunted. He is slurring into his cell phone.

The mind is seeing the academic chatting up his colleague. It is seeing a miserable tale of city-planning madness and misplaced home-building ambition being made into light, fluffy coffee table conversation. It is seeing how that one coffee has extended itself into a daily chat that the staffroom seems to have accepted. Right now, the academic is thinking of how riveting Malati Patel finds his take on the history of Delhi. The tale of Gurgaon's urban lunacy could be his next 'coffee topic' with Malati. Yes, they've already had three 'coffee dates', each longer than the last, and each time she has warmed up to him a little more. He can now imagine her shining eyes as she listens, the way her throat moves up and down as she throws her head back to laugh at his latest humorous profundity, the way her breasts thrust against the fabric of her dress when she is sitting across him, eyes to the ceiling, buffeted by gusts of helpless laughter at his brilliant sallies on the levels of certifiable insanity in the planning of Delhi's pretender. The all-seeing whisky-sharpened mind is seeing all this.

Perhaps, one last whisky will clarify on which hillside the flowers will bloom?

🏠

Day 106

$\mathcal{T}$HE AIR COOLERS in the staffroom have been turned on. The five pleasant days that make for spring in Delhi are over and done with. The march of seasons is assuming a quickstep. Soon, the days will be welded together in a blurred haze of heat and dust. Similarly, events in our life too seem to have speeded up.

Roshni and I are back to being on amicable terms. As one tearfully and the other enthusiastically agreed, nothing had really happened. A baseless accusation followed by equally baseless insults. One cancelling the other out, or so is the easy assumption. There is however an uneasy reality beneath this. There are undercurrents in our relationship now…swirling dark waters that seem to throw up the debris of every past fight onto the sunny sandbanks of our current life. It's as if everything of the previous decade is now being dredged up from the depths and laid bare to a harsh inquisitor's piercing light. New meanings are emerging from long buried quarrels. New slights are being imagined from old hurts. And everything is being flimsily papered over with good manners and stilted formality.

On the surface, however, a resigned routine reigns—from home to college and back for me. It's the last few days before the summer holidays begin. Roshni has never followed a routine; sometimes, it's a hectic seven non-stop days and nights of working and sometimes it's a fortnight of relaxing, working on designs at home, gardening and exercising. So, each is back to doing what they did before and following the posters that have suddenly sprouted all over—an English crown with the message 'Keep Calm and Carry On'. There's one up on the staffroom wall as well and it's on the table under it that I am organizing my Indian History (Freedom Struggle) notes.

'Oh! Developed a taste for literature now, have we? You do know he's a Nobel Laureate now? Don't tell me you don't?'

Too late! Malati Patel has already seen the book that FatBum had thrust into my hands so many months ago. Truth to tell, I was quite enjoying reading it and that's why maybe it was in my college bag.

'Actually, this is something my landlord presented me when he got to know that we were, you know, buying that place in Gurgaon.'

'Quite a guy he must be then, your landlord? Amazingly sensitive of him, must say. To be appreciating Naipaul in this day and age…nice. Reads a lot, does he?'

Malati and I have reached our usual place by the coffee machine and the last question has been tossed over her shoulder while bending slightly to stir the sugar into her own coffee. While I am debating whether to answer in the affirmative or in the negative, I cannot help but make a silent academic observation—today it is a pair of Levi's that is taking up the strain…and taking it up beautifully.

'No, actually, he's not much of a reader. And sensitive? To sulpha drugs maybe.'

'If he's not a reader, how did he present you with this book while you are eaten up with your house-building mission? You do realize that this is either a massive fluke or a wonderfully sensitive piece of thoughtful gifting?'

'Malati, you have to meet Mr Khanna to realize that this

is neither a fluke nor thoughtful. It's just, well, just a piece of out of context tradition.'

'Tell me, how much of this have you actually read? Let's spend some time talking about the book, your landlord and also about your blessed Gurgaon flat.'

This time we talk for four coffees and two classes. The two classes are just the interrupters of our coffees and conversations. I would never have thought Malati (strangely thinking of her now without remembering tightly stretched jeans or straining tops) capable of such depths. The way she takes me through the travails of the poor old and the poor young Mohun Biswas is a real eye-opener. I guess I will have to read the book again. She is also drawing insidious parallels between our journeys, but then, I draw her attention to the fact that broken-down old-frame houses in abandoned sugar plantations in the Caribbean is actually a very different proposition from modern condo units in earthquake-resistant skyscrapers located in bustling international metropolises. At which point, she laughs, pats me on the arm and reminds me that she knows my views on the 'bustling international metropolis', and points out that maybe building a house in an abandoned sugar field would actually make more sense. At least there, there would be no pretenses...no pretenses towards being urbanized, or having modern facilities, etc. And, isn't life really better without pretense?

This is when we decide to drop all pretenses and admit frankly to each other that we enjoy our conversations and should perhaps talk more. However, to prevent the unavoidable wagging of tongues were we to do it in the staffroom again, we agree to meet outside. She tells me she knows of a private little place for coffee in Khan Market. I tell her that I will meet her there at 11.30 a.m. next Wednesday. Of course, it is only to prevent the absolutely unnecessary and unwarranted scandals that the petty minds of our colleagues would conjure up that we have decided to meet outside. Otherwise, what's wrong with the staffroom coffee?

As I am stuck in traffic on the way home, I realize that today is the first day in many weeks that I haven't been miserable throughout the day thinking of Roshni and myself. Today is the first day that I haven't been consumed with worry about the loan and the stupid brouhaha about an extra charge—the EDC (External Development Charge) if you please—that the builder has now decided to levy on us. Today is the first day in, perhaps, years that I am attempting to sing along with the FM radio in the car.

The traffic clears as I turn left to catch the Outer Ring Road. I am in the slow lane, both literally and figuratively, enjoying the views of the Deer Park and the City Forest that line the road, while idly fantasizing about what the future could be, when, suddenly, I see a sight that takes me back a full decade and a half. It is perhaps a fairly commonplace sight... A young man pushing a motorcycle with a flat tyre up the road, accompanied by a young lady, perhaps his girlfriend.

In a flash, I am transported back to a conversation of fifteen years ago between Roshni and me. I am forced to pull over to the side of the road and stop the car.

I remember asking, 'You mean you actually had a cow at home.'

'It was no big deal, you know. It was after all Vakil saab's home. He was a stickler for fresh cow milk and he always got what he wanted. I called him Baoji. Everyone called him Baoji.'

'But he wasn't really your father?'

'Of course not. Technically, he was my grandfather. But, he was simply Baoji. Everybody called him that and so did I. After all, I came into that household as a six-month-old baby.

My mother was the eldest daughter and she was the *manhus*, the unlucky one, who according to her mother-in-law was the one who swallowed up her husband's life.'

I remember clearly my palms starting to sweat at this and the bike almost slipping from my grasp. Damn that Diptesh Jha and his stupidly unreliable motorcycle with tyres as bald as Professor Dutta's head. Trust him to lend me this begging-to-be-punctured 'Dobbin' when I asked everyone in the hostel for a bike for my 'serious' date.

'Manhus?'

'My father died when I was four months old. I don't know how. Nobody ever told me. It was a road accident, I think. My mother was unscathed. Her mother-in-law, who already disliked her, started a systematic programme of abuse against her *manhus* daughter-in-law. This continued until the Vakil saab stepped in and took his daughter and granddaughter back home.'

'Vakil saab, eh! a.k.a Baoji. What was he like? Progressive and liberal?'

'Not in the least. Well, not in the sense that "progressive" and "liberal" is understood today. But human values are human values, regardless of the time, and those he had aplenty. He was an out and out Punjabi man who came to Meerut as a penniless student after partition. He supported his family, studied law and ultimately became the "Vakil saab" of the entire neighbourhood. Yes, nobody, especially women, dared raise their voice in his presence. All women had to have a dupatta over their heads. Meals would be served to him without his asking, his shoes would be taken off as soon as he came home and sat down, his word was the law... He was the complete patriarch, yes. But no, he would not tolerate any bullying or unfairness. He always insisted that everyone, even all the girls, got educated and ensured that nobody ever left his home with an empty belly or empty pockets. That was Baoji.'

'So, all this English-speaking and fashion designing was encouraged by him then?'

'Are you kidding? All this was my *mausi*'s doing. You'd love to meet her.'

'Mausi?'

'My mother's youngest sister, Baoji's youngest daughter. She was sixteen and taking her Higher Secondary Exams when I came into the family. She brought me up, since my mother, to justify her place in the house, was always busy managing the household. So, I became KK Mausi's charge.'

I had never known a girl with such an interesting story before. Well, honestly, it's not as if I had known dozens of girls before. But here I was, in my final year of MA and there was this drop-dead pretty and yet somehow a completely unassuming girl from Meerut studying fashion designing in Delhi who was keeping pace with me as we both sweated our way to a tyre puncture repair shop. We had met three times before at parties with common friends. This was the first time that I had invited her out alone and it had started disastrously with the rear tyre blowing out within ten minutes of my starting the ride from her hostel to the 'Osaka' restaurant where we were supposed to have a 'Chinese' meal.

KK Mausi turned out to be Kumkum Mausi, the most spirited and feisty of Baoji's daughters. She was a girl who hated middle-class Meerut, the Hindi-medium school and, what she called, the Hindi-medium life. She was also the girl who married for love and settled in Mumbai with her advertising executive husband. Also, she was the mausi who loved Roshni like a younger sister and swore to change her life.

'She was the first person I saw standing up to Baoji's roaring. I was in class VIII and mausi came down from Mumbai, took me out of the Hindi-medium school, enrolled me in an English-medium convent, got my ponytails cut into a bob and bought me two pairs of jeans and T-shirts…all in a single day. And then, she told Baoji to move with the times!'

'You know, she's really the reason why I am here. In Delhi, I mean. And, studying fashion designing. She forced me out of Meerut. She wants me to see the world, meet some interesting people, do some interesting stuff.'

It was after the meal, after the fortune cookies were cracked open at Osaka that I realized that this girl's story would take me a lifetime to read.

It is only after I park the car this evening, only after my last smoke that I ask myself, when did I stop reading her story? When did I start reading the advertising blurbs of another story?

Day 127

TWO WEEKS AGO, Roshni accused me of 'getting stranger'. When I enquired after her grammar in my best supercilious, designed to irritate, pompous manner, she did not blow up as she seems wont to nowadays. She just settled back, made herself smaller in the seat, looked out of the window and said, 'You were always strange. Now, you're getting stranger. Earlier, it used to be so endearing, this strangeness. Now, it's, at most times, irritating and sometimes, just hateful.'

This was late at night and we were returning from our Bengali clan 'get-together' in Chittaranjan Park. I did not even bother to respond. I just rolled down the window and smoked a cigarette in injured silence.

Our clan 'adda'—the Bengali 'get-together'—is a family tradition started by my older brother, Tubluda. He is the brains and the success of the family—a professional entrepreneur settled in San Jose, California, USA. He started off as a simple dentist and now owns a string of orthodontic clinics spread all over the West Coast. The unfortunate habit of giving wildly inappropriate Bengali nicknames seems particularly misplaced in his case. He is four inches taller than me which makes him six foot two and forty kilos heavier. Now, imagine this large, serious, portly, bald and eminently respectable white-coat wearing professional, Dr Bishwajeet, being suddenly reduced to a 'Tublu', a name that is immediately reminiscent of short pants, sleeveless vests and grubby palms clutching marbles. Tubluda has of course Americanized this too…like he has everything else. So, now, it's either Dr Bish or TwoBlue, as in meetdr2blue@gmail.com—that's my older brother.

Dada left for the US early, much before I came to Delhi, and has now lived there for the best part of a quarter century. Nostalgia, in his case, is directly proportional to distance and time, and the further both move, the more nostalgic he seems to become. However, his yearning is for an India that does not exist anymore and unfortunately even his microcosmic slice of it—the Bengaliness of Chittaranjan Park—is not what it used to be. Before he left for the US, Tubluda spent six weeks in I Block, Chittranjan Park as a 'paying guest'. His memories date from that time and had he the choice he would have bottled them up in a time capsule and luxuriated in them during his annual pilgrimages to India. Chittranjan Park, or EPDP colony as he still calls it, was the original East Pakistan Displaced Peoples colony of New Delhi. It was a place for the settlement of all the Bengalis who, after the partition of India, came in from erstwhile East Pakistan, now Bangladesh. Delhi, with what nowadays seems like uncharacteristic hospitality, had in the first few years after independence, accommodated and settled waves of refugees in its 'extensions'. The Western Extension Area, WEA or Karol Bagh, became home to the Punjabis. The same happened with South Extension and promptly, both these areas became markets. Defence Colony was handed over to the intrepid servicemen who could brave the wilderness south of Lodi Colony and it was the rocky and barren ground, south east of South Extension that offered a virgin territory for the settlement of the unsettled Bengalis of East Pakistan. Thus, the EPDP colony came into being and was soon named after one of the eminent sons of undivided Bengal, a proud nation builder—Deshbandhu Chittaranjan Das.

Chittaranjan Park, at least till Tubluda's paying guest days, was a completely Bengali society, for the most part. You could actually, and people routinely did, get by without speaking a word of English or Hindi. Even the signs were in Bengali and between Markets 1 and 2, everything that a Bengali needed—from music and magazines to fish and mustard and everything in-between—was readily available. It was nothing out of the ordinary to see people walking around wearing white dhotis and carrying black umbrellas with adda sessions happening on every available bench. This was the world that Tubluda wanted to return to every year, but, every year it would change a little more. And every year, he would try a little harder to recreate it. Every year, the 'Dillification' of CR Park would increase by degrees—Mr Mukherjee would pass away, his children would settle abroad and the house would be sold to Mr Arora; Mrs Sengupta could use a little extra cash and really, who needs such a big house? Plus that Ahluwalia builder is offering a flat too with all that money for the same plot; Rathin Das cannot make a business success out of his Bengali book and music store so why not just sell out to Banwari Lal Chemists and Medicos? And, then these students—yes, of course, they come from all over India—but, hey, they make such good tenants. Year by year, little by little, CR Park would change. And, every year, with a progressively more pronounced American accent, Tubluda would try to change it back for those two weeks that were his India pilgrimage. One can well imagine a huffing and puffing tubby, bald-headed, bespectacled football player manoeuvring the ball up to the goalposts only to find that they've shifted again.

Finally, after a decade of this, Tubluda decided to cement the posts. He bought a house in CR Park and, in a stroke of unwitting irony, rented out the ground floor to a family from Bihar and the second floor to a perfectly delightful Keralite couple. The first floor is where he decided to bottle his memories, that is, create a shrine for the 'Bangali para', the 'Bengali colony' he had used as his launching pad for his American Dream. And it was this first-floor flat that became the 'venue' for our annual 'get-togethers', a place for our Bengali 'adda' sessions.

It's actually quite a nice little flat... Two bedrooms and a study, plus, of course, the combined drawing-dining room and a fairly big and spacious kitchen. Built in the late 1970s, it is definitely showing its age but for the museum that it is, that's absolutely appropriate. Tubluda used to keep it locked up for 11 months a year, leaving only the servants' quarters open. Five years ago, Kantu *Pishemoshai*, my uncle by marriage, was hit by the Dakshineshwar Esplanade Bus No. 32 in Kolkata. An aged man, he toppled off his equally aged LML Vespa scooter and never really got up again. Ratna *Pishi*, his wife and our late father's youngest sister, suddenly found herself widowed. In quick succession, she found herself homeless and penniless too. Pishemoshai, an Accounts 'Officer' in a private firm in Kolkata, never really had the means or the vision to set up a retirement fund and he certainly could not invest in a home of his own. They moved from small to smaller rented houses across Kolkata, living a life of quiet desperation, like many of that generation, depending on their son for their golden years. That worthy lad passed through the stages of gloriously talented singer to unbearably conceited egomaniac, to hopeless alcoholic, to drug addict, to charged for theft under-trial, to finally grinding to a full stop with suicide. Sonless, husbandless, homeless and penniless, Ratna Pishi entered the sixth decade of her hitherto fairly joyless life.

Tubluda was, of course, monitoring all this from sunny

California. I think he has a software in place to do all this—just like he manages his clinics which seem to breed like rabbits and remain as healthy as horses—he manages all the family affairs with the same pinpoint accuracy and professional excellence. In his diagram of duties and responsibilities, of needs and desires, of the good thing to do and the good thing to have, here was suddenly a binary correspondence. The zero had met the one and his computer clicked on. Ratna Pishi needs a place, my place needs a caretaker...Bingo! All the lights turned green, the siren went off and the letters on the one-armed bandit spelled JACKPOT!

Ratna Pishi was duly imported from Kolkata and installed in the CR Park flat. Tubluda was duly showered with praise and the house duly cared for. 'I always knew there was something about him. He is the son I never had. Tublu is a diamond, pure diamond. God bless him to live forever!'

It was the perfect symbiosis. Tubluda had found the ideal keeper of his museum and Ratna Pishi had found a new lease of life. She stepped into this second innings of her housekeeping game with a flourish and took over the reins as if she was to the manor born. With maybe three words of Hindi, two of English, no clothes except saris, no knowledge and lesser interest of anything that was not Bengali, she was the ideal champion of Tubluda's 'Preserve Bengal' movement. The only person who chafed, and foolishly made his displeasure clear at this arrangement, was the servant lad who had, until now, ruled in solitary splendour. Ratna Pishi, displaying a political acumen, a grasp of strategy and a plain vindictiveness that, I, for one, had never suspected her of, mounted siege on the poor lad's position. Long-distance telephone calls and frequent appeals to the plight of a poor hapless widow were her weapons of choice. As a last resort, the nuclear bomb of tears coupled with 'what would *Borda*, his father, have said of this situation, I do not know' was also deployed. It was an unequal fight. Tukai, with his ten-year-old VIP suitcase, short pants, rubber slippers and a collection of Grateful Dead and Deep Purple T-shirts (the last, a symbol of Tubluda's bachelor days) was sent packing in two months' time. Many applicants were screened and a widow, Mampi *Mashi*, of impeccable background from Krishna Nagar, Nadia District, West Bengal was found worthy of being Ratna Pishi's live-in help. Now, Pishi was ready to begin her life afresh.

This was five years ago. And I cannot help but marvel at the change that time and a changed situation have wrought. From a quivering mass of under confidence and prone to bursting into tears at the slightest provocation, Ratna Pishi is now an impeccably turned-out, starched sari-wearing, completely confident and dignified, indeed bossy, old lady. Her long list of health issues have all disappeared as has her diffidence about speaking. Now, being able to speak only in Bengali, and in better Bengali than anyone around her, has become a mark of honour, not a cause for embarrassed silence. She has gradually moved from being a refugee in the house to its de facto owner and this, like nothing else before, seems to have empowered her. Tubluda, who, when he first played this master stroke, used to preen about 'the human businessman' that he is, now seems, frankly nonplussed. On one of the evenings during this visit of his, he was marvelling at how she told him off about the different kinds of rice that are required in any household. 'You, of course, are all children, you can't be expected to know all of this'—was what she closed the one-sided conversation with.

Tubluda was left spluttering with an asphyxiated indignation as he recounted the incident to Roshni and me while he put away his third Californian Chardonnay, 'I can't be expected to know all this? Hell! I can certainly be expected to pay for it though!'

This was the context of the weekend get-together that Roshni and I were returning from on that evening. Increasingly, these were now presided over by Ratna Pishi with Tubluda relegated to a supporting role as the signer of the cheques. I felt really bad for my brother as the reality of this situation was moving further and further away from his original vision of the Bengali family get-together. First, it was not really Bengali. Unlike the earlier days, when the audience was homogenously Bengali, now some of the spouses, like mine for instance, were not Bengali. Also, the children, even when both parents were Bengali, were definitely not native speakers of the language. Second, it was not really a family affair anymore.

Tubluda and his wife were going through 'a difficult period'. Divorce was, of course, out of the question as the assets were too many and neither party wanted to risk litigation. So, his wife and he came to India at different times of the year; like everything else, they took their vacations separately. Their children, like many of the children in the extended family, had grown up and grown away. They could not be bothered with spending a claustrophobic weekend in the hottest period of the year in a polluted city with a bunch of aged relatives whose sole topic of conversation seemed to be 'the good old days'. Third, it was hardly a get-together anymore. It was an incendiary mix of unfriendly relatives speaking in babel of tongues and their sole reason for coming together was the fact that Tubluda was known to be obscenely wealthy and each person hoped that there would be something to be gained out of this annual punishment.

The only person who seemed to blossom in all of this was Ratna Pishi. This was her big moment, these were the weeks that she spent the rest of the year preparing for, this was the time that her house was to be showed off to its best advantage and her superiority in everything Bengali to be stamped over all the relatives that she had spent a lifetime in the shadow of. Such was the magic of the house—it made a star of the person who lived in it and reduced to dross the dreams of the person who paid for it. Tubluda's physical goalpost had become the chain that dragged him down while his dreams remained an uncatchable remove away. Obviously, buying a house and then installing the perfect housekeeper did not work as the dreamcatcher for him.

'Quite the dragon lady she's become, hasn't she?' I asked him as I flicked the ash from my cigarette out of the balcony railing into the downstairs sit-out—a habit that the Bihari family, the first tenants downstairs, had so bitterly complained about on many previous occasions.

'Uff, she and that blasted Mampi Mashi! They are a duo of tyrannical old biddies if there ever was one. Three pujas we've had in the past four days. Bloody house is still full of incense smoke. Remember, how the kids used to spend the days playing carom in the olden times? And "dark room" at nights? Where are those kids? And where have those days and nights gone? We'd all be singing Hemanta songs together at this time, now, this crowd doesn't even know much Bengali, forget the songs.'

Going back to that evening. Tubluda and I are outside on the balcony. The 'get-together' is still getting together at the dining table. Three kinds of fish, various dals, and the quintessentially Bengali preparations like *chocchodis* and *shuktos* are being waded through. We are taking a break and will rejoin the crowd inside later for the *payesh* and *shondesh*, the 'genuinely Bengali' sweets.

'Well, no kids anymore. They are all grown up and have gone away. Anyway, I never had any of my own.'

'Yeah. Sometimes, I think you are the wise one. No kids, no businesses, no houses—yeah, that's the smart thing to do. There is nothing to tie you down. You go where your dreams take you, eh? Smart. That's really smart. Travel light, all through life.'

At this, I nearly choked on the cigarette. Smart? He's talking about me? Funny, I'd never thought of myself that way. I always thought that I did not have any of the above, simply because I could not afford it, certainly not because I did not want it.

'Look where I am stuck with this. I can't stay, I can't get out. Not that I really enjoy sweating out these two weeks here anymore. But, hey! I can't really pull out my anchors either. I certainly can't sell out, what's going to happen to the old biddies then, eh? The only thing is it doesn't really cost me anything. I mean, in the scheme of things, it doesn't cost anything. But let me tell you one thing—never do anything for free for anyone. The more people are obligated to you, the more they dislike you. Charity should only be a one-time thing, and not a thing that you need to keep feeding continuously at one end because at the other end, boy, you are going to get shit. You think Ratna Pishi likes me? No, she doesn't. And the truth is that she only dislikes me because she is obligated to me, because she depends on me for her monthly fund transfers and because she knows I have really no reason to keep doing that. It's her insecurity that's making her so bossy. That's why I say, boy, never do anything for free for anyone.'

We walk back into the dining room where Ratna Pishi and Mampi Mashi are now laying out the sweets. A calorific overload that the middle-aged members of the get-together could very well do without. But Ratna Pishi has to go the whole nine yards and everybody grins and bears it—indeed chews it down—because they all know that Tubluda is a whale for tradition and who knows what munificence may be bestowed if he is retained in good humour. After all, in that gaggle of relatives and hangers-on, there are those with children who *could* be studying in America, those whose standing would get a significant boost were they to wangle a large donation for this year's Durga Puja, those who were looking for free stay and transport during their West Coast holidays and also those who were in the race simply for the exotic gifts that he always brought on these trips. And then, there were those like me, who had the inside track on the blackness of his current mood... But what is this? Suddenly, I see my beautiful wife trying to catch my eye, wanting to talk to me. Actually, she is excusing herself from the table and casually walking me into one of the bedrooms. What is this? Am I about to get lucky? That too in a houseful of people? Now, that'll be new, on many counts.

'Did you ask him?'

'Ask him? Who? What?!'

'Ask that brother of yours of course... Croesus himself, the king Kuber? When I saw the two of you getting cozy on the balcony, I thought you'd pop the question. It was good timing. So, what did he say?'

'Say what about what Roshni? I'm afraid you're losing me.'

'You mean you hobnobbed with him for fifteen minutes alone, with nobody to disturb the two of you, and even then you did not ask him?'

'Did not ask him what?'

'Did not ask him to loan you the extra 5 lakhs that will now be required for the house! After all we talked about in the car, after how I prepared you, you forgot everything?! So, what did you talk about then? Those sweet old days of short pants and Phantom comics? Or those times of load-shedding and water shortages? Or how you used to get new clothes only on Durga Puja, once a year? Or about all the same things you've already talked a million times? Uff! You're really strange. I wonder why I put up with all this!'

Roshni leaves and the door bangs shut behind her. Obviously, she is going straight to the bathroom to make up and prepare her face to meet the other made-up faces at the dining table. Obviously, I will hear a lot more doors being banged in the near future. And to think that I was briefly entertaining thoughts of getting lucky! Equally obviously, she is right. After all, that is why we are here. That is what we are all here for. What was I thinking of when I was excluding myself from the others and their reasons for 'getting together'. Sorry, not 'their', 'our' reasons, our reasons for getting together are all the same—personal gain without much effort and certainly no obligation. But now, after having heard Tubluda on the terrace and knowing what he thinks, how am I going to bring up my completely unsecured loan application? He's just been waxing eloquent on never doing anything for free for anyone anymore. Obviously, I cannot bring it up. If so, I have no reason to stay here. After all, we are not here for conviviality and good cheer, we are here for a purpose. If that purpose cannot be achieved, why linger?

Translating thought into action takes but a moment for a driven achiever like myself. The bedroom door opens, I get out, announce to the collected audience that for us the get-together is over, request Roshni to accompany me, open the front door and get out. There's no one who can quite achieve the fuck-up of an evening like I can. Sometimes, I am quite the overachiever.

From 'endearing' to 'irritating' to 'just hateful'—my strangeness has travelled the full spectrum for Roshni. However, by the time we reach home, I am at peace. Yes, I am getting stranger. Be that as it may because for some, that strangeness is still endearing. Or how did Malati describe it the one time we had coffee at Khan Market? Ahh, that I have 'a certain mystique'. Yes, that's what she called it. 'You have a certain mystique.

Its sounds clichéd, but you seem to march to the beat of a different drum.'

Clichéd? Perhaps. But, my dear Malati, it is nice nonetheless. Or maybe she meant I was just plain bananas? Stark raving mad? Maybe both mean the same thing?

Day 148

THE SUN IS shining in the sky. What a typically English statement! With all its connotations of happiness, good cheer and general well-being, this is truly a beautiful English statement to describe a truly beautiful, if rare, English weather condition. This, however, is India in the latter half of June. More specifically, the plains of North India, and most specifically, one of the most polluted cities of the world. Here, English is stretched to its linguistic limits to describe the pitiless, relentless scorching that the sun inflicts on the world at this time. 'Shining' is far too benevolent a word, and inaccurate too. Everything is flash-fried by an angry glowering sky. The source of heat and light is indistinct. The sun does not shine as a clear and separate entity. Multiple layers of permanently suspended pollutants diffuse and refract both its heat and light and it is as if the whole sky is aflame and is cooking the Earth below in high heat like a gigantic inverted cooking range. Move to the shade, and the knob on this range gets turned from 'high heat' to 'simmer', or from 'hi' to 'sim'. There is not a drop of moisture in the air and waves of dry dust scour every exposed surface like sandpaper. The hundreds of square kilometres of paving, asphalt and concrete that have replaced the trees, grassy open plains and mossy ponds of once-upon-a-time rural Delhi, strike back with equal ferocity to this daily abuse. Throughout the night they exhale back the heat they receive during the day as if challenging the pitiless daytime skies—'see, we can give it back to you too. Our turn comes at night'. Caught between this cruel and unremitting exchange of these hammer-blows of heat is every living being of this city. And yet, life continues. Indeed, flying in the face of all logic, it thrives. Living and loving will always find a way.

'How is it that the monsoons are delayed every year? I mean, if they are delayed so consistently, doesn't it stand to reason that the Met Department change the "expected date" to what they now call the "delayed date"? I mean shouldn't the expected date of the monsoon in Delhi now be mid-July and not end-June?'

Malati is back from her Scandinavian holiday, a twelve-night Baltic cruise with her husband and his Swedish business partner. This was preceded by a week in Copenhagen and Stockholm. She had left soon after the college closed for the summer vacations and has returned only two days ago, plunging straight from the frigid and crystal clear waters of the Baltic into the simmering cauldron that is Delhi. Little wonder then, that she is thirsting for whatever relief the monsoon may bring.

'I tell you what—enough of these coffees. It's just too hot in any case. Let's just have a chilled beer.'

'Why stop at one?' I reply, signalling the waiter.

'One at a time Mr B, one at a time. And, one thing at a time.'

We are, once again, in Khan Market. Coming into the lane between two markets that command some of the world's highest commercial real estate prices and showcase the globe's most iconic brands is like entering a different world altogether. It's a narrow cobbled street that runs as a spine along the U-bend whose two sides, the inner U and the outer U—without getting metaphysical—are home to the stores. Small shops are lined along the walls of the inner lane as well and every few yards there are punctuations in these walls that open up to steep staircases which penetrate the recesses of the first floors above these shops. These were originally the residences of the shopkeepers and all of them now, almost without exception, have been converted into chic eateries, coffee shops and lounge bars. Malati and I met first at a place that overlooked the outer U. Now, we are at a place that overlooks the inner U. Maybe, there is meaning in this too.

'Cheers! Do tell me about your trip.'

'Cheers. What's there to say? It's like all the brochures and websites advertise—find peace while at sea and all that. I've done this before you know, and frankly, I get bored. Only that the weather is so incredible and everything is so neat, clean and organized. Coming back here, even for an Indian like me, is a bit of a shock. But that's enough about me. You tell me, how is your house coming along? The house for my Mr Biswas.'

At this, she lays a proprietorial hand over my forearm. Over long staffroom conversations and two coffee shop meetings, I have, apparently, become 'her' Mr Biswas. Such is the appropriation of those who come to life with a well-secured sense of entitlement. No doubt, 'amazing scenes' will soon be witnessed, perhaps in this very restaurant.

Whose home was this I wonder? The lounge where we are now sitting and thirstily drinking beer. It was the house of which Mr Khan? Which refugee from the North West Frontier Province was granted this particular unit to make or remake his fortunes in this new city of New Delhi? After all, Khan Market, named after the brother of the famed Khan Abdul Ghaffar Khan— the less famous Khan Abdul Jabbar Khan—was the site for the resettlement of the people of that province. Which tall Pathan family lived first in this dwelling? And climbed tiredly into it after a busy day at the shop below? What stories would these walls tell if one could but go beneath the kitschy posters that now adorn them? What moving tales of sacrifice and savings would one hear if one could shut off the Dire Straits track now playing at a loud volume? Was there a bedroom here? What nights of steamy passion did this floor bear witness to? Or maybe it was duty delivered? Was it over here that the next generation was conceived? The generation that would make this shopkeeping-backwater the lodestone of the expatriate population of Delhi. Was Pushtu spoken and understood within these four walls? And what would those hardy Pathans say or understand, I wonder, of the tawdry little affairs that are enacted here every day... furtively, fumblingly, tucked away from the glare of the noonday sun and bathed in the cool foaming green of liberating beer.

Of course, I do not say any of this. That would be moving the strangeness quotient of the 'mystique' laden Mr B into the 'irritating' or 'hateful' zone. That would be a huge strategic error. However, I must stick as close as possible to my character as that makes it the most convincing. So, the strangeness must be there, but only so much and no more. Don't they say that the most convincing lies are the ones closest to the truth?

'Your Mr Biswas's house is coming along just fine. Roshni and I went and saw it a week ago. The foundation is laid and the underground parking now has a roof. The apartment block is up to ground level. However, I wonder...'

Here, I take a significant pause and draw in a deep breath, building up the strangeness quotient. Malati leans forward to listen. We are still new-enough friends for one to actually make an effort to listen to the other. We still wait for the other to finish a sentence or to complete a thought.

'I wonder what its fate will be. Will it become a happy home? Or an unhappy house? Will it be a warm haven or a suffocating prison? Or will it become like this?' I gesture around, 'Some pretentious restaurant with the half-life of an unstable uranium isotope.'

Bull's-eye! The strangeness quotient has rocked the metre. This is a hit. Malati leans back, flicks the hair over her eyes, crosses her arms across her front and regards me with a frank inquisitiveness. She is wearing loose pyjama pants with a matching pink racerback top. Over this, in deference to the Delhi heat, she had thrown a filmy patterned cotton stole. In here, however, there is no heat and so the stole is off, lying in a crumpled heap on the chair next to her. Her arms are crossed under her breasts, the material of her top is stretched tightly, she is sitting directly under the air conditioner, and I cannot help but notice the two studs that are appearing under the flimsy material of the top, directly over her wrists.

'You are an interesting man, Mr B. You know, during our Miranda House hostel days, we used to call it turning on the headlights. But don't flatter yourself. You're not that interesting yet, it's just the cold blast from the AC.'

The next two hours are very interesting. Now that the topic is raised; now that the dam is breached (and I am sure amateur psychologists would find the turn of phrase to be revelatory), it seems that there is no stopping the flood. It's amazing how much of an icebreaker the mere awareness of puckered nipples can be. The profundities of homes and the struggles of people acquiring and living in them, be it the refugees of Khan Market or the indentured labourers of Mr Biswas's neighbourhood, are derailed. Malati and I, well, to be honest, mainly Malati, talks about her growing-up days in Delhi. We talk about that one topic that seems to have a disproportionate share in the minds of most people, whether growing up or grown-up—sex. We talk a lot about sex. It is an endlessly interesting topic. However, our approach to it and its availability to us seem to be at two ends of a spectrum—for one, infra and for the other, ultra.

Malati was not always a Patel. She grew up as Malati Malhotra in one of those quarter acre bungalows in W Block Greater Kailash I, a tony South Delhi Colony that in her growing-up years was definitely one of the toniest. Huge manicured lawns, armies of servants, every kind of British Raj hangover possible—only replace the Mountbatten with the Malhotra—and of course money, oozing out of every pore.

'What do you think it was like? It's a classic story. Everyone's heard it a million times before. Grandfather was one of the first Indians in the UN, that's why the plots in Jorbagh, GK 1, Anand Lok, Panchsheel, etc. My father, the great Aseem Malhotra, was a truly limitless man. Limitless in his ability to generate money, to be offensive to everyone around and of course to give love...to all his female employees, his friends' wives, his far-flung relatives, hell, even the maids in the house, everyone except his own wife. Basically, he was one big fucker. Ultimately, of course, he was the one who got screwed. His business partners humped him over and he had to sell off the Jorbagh house—the pride and joy of his growing-up years. Or so he'd have us believe. Not like him to be sentimental over something like a house and not that it changed him in the least, he is still the most odious man you'd rather not meet. Only now, he is an odious invalid. You do smoke, don't you? Why don't you lend me one and ask that fellow to leave us another beer here?'

The restaurant's management has thoughtfully provided a sunshade over the open smoking area and has installed a desert cooler that offers some welcome relief from the summer's heat as we light up.

'I had just turned fourteen. I mean that's how old I was when I first smoked. Rothmans. Shefali and I had taken a single cigarette from Papa's packet lying by his bedside table and had run out to smoke it in the vegetable patch behind the kitchen. The packet said "King Size" and "By Special Appointment". I remember laughing uncontrollably because Shefali said that if King Size means that this is the size of the British King's you-know-what, then, I feel sorry for him. She laughed louder when I said I felt sorrier for the queen. I stopped smoking only when I started teaching in this college.'

Here I was nodding intelligently and smiling at the right places all the while thinking how completely different my life was and whether sharing would be the appropriate thing to do; or whether sharing would make the perception needle shift from 'strange' to maybe, I don't know, 'pathetic'? Would she then start regarding me as something out of a Satyajit Ray film, a *Pather Panchali* kind of character? How would a cigarette-smoking, party-going, miniskirt-wearing, GK 1-living girl of a super-rich, big-fucker father even identify with a good middle-class Bengali lad who at 'just turned fourteen' still oiled his hair and dutifully rolled his sacred thread around his ear before taking a shit?

'Thank you…and you can turn the music up again now,' Malati said to the waiter as she settled down in her seat again.

'You know why they named me "Malati"? After all, it is not normally the kind of name you'd associate with a Punjabi, would you? It's more of a Bengali name, *na*? Something you'd know about more, maybe there's even a Malati in your history somewhere? Some Bengali bombshell?'

'No, no, not in my history. But in my future perhaps?'

There you go! If not in actions, at least I can be adventurous with my words. 'But do tell me—why "Malati"?'

'It was because of my mother. She was a Sanskrit teacher at the Andrews Ganj Kendriya Vidalaya. Imagine what a misfit she must have been in that staffroom; more than me in our staffroom, I think. Imagine getting dropped off at the gates of a government school in a Mercedes or a Land Cruiser. In the winters, she invariably walked home. Papa always felt insulted by her profession, always thought it was below our 'status', always thought she worked there to spite him. He wanted her to be a socialite, you know, have lunches at the Taj and things like that. But, Mummy stuck to her guns. She never gave up that job of hers. I think it kept her sane, considering that Papa absolutely and completely ignored her. I honestly think he loved her only twice with two spectacularly damaged results—Shefali and me. After that, he kept her at home like he kept all his other possessions. His permanently priapic passions were vented on other objects with holes. I told you mine is a classic story. I warned you before that it's so classic, it's boring. It's been multiplied into the hundreds of households all over Delhi's bungalows. Only difference is that there the women also get their share, patrolling South Extension for the men on hire. Mummy, instead, sublimated all her frustrations and disappointments into Sanskrit and Hindi poetry. '

I can see that Malati is getting maudlin. I need to steer the conversation back to an easier track. While women picking up men for hire in South Ex are definitely interesting, I am genuinely more eager to know why she was named Malati.

'So, why Malati?'

'Because of the Jasmine tree which grew outside the bedroom where I was conceived. It must have been a rare happy night for my mother. Apparently, the one thing she remembered the most about those nights was the fragrance of Jasmine. And, the moment she saw me, she knew, even though I was only a howling infant, that I would be the one to spread this fragrance all around. Papa, of course, was not interested. Apparently the only thing he said was, "another girl huh!" and then went off to Thailand with his friends to celebrate.'

Seeing my somewhat befuddled state, she poked me in the nose and said, 'Malati is Sanskrit for Jasmine, my dear professor of History.'

I sense a break in this sentimental journey and know that it's time to press home the advantage. Yes, I know it's sad and it's tragic how monetary affluence does not equate with happiness and how pseudo-chauvinistic Indian men have traditionally not been the world's greatest fathers and husbands and how this has permanently damaged and scarred entire generations...yes, I know all that, but then, so does everybody else and it is all so everyday that it is frankly not even tragic anymore. It is the story of too many homes across every imaginable spectrum of society. The amazing and endlessly creative nature of human's animal-survival instinct has adjusted to this maladjusted male and found a way. Malati's journey was interesting and I wanted to hear more about it. I wanted to know which way she had led her life's journey. As for the 'whys', or the motivators and the triggers of that journey, well, the psychiatrists and social scientists were welcome to analyse all that.

'So, how and where did the fragrance of this Jasmine spread?'

'Strange, huh? Mummy's obsession with fragrance and flowers? To name the elder daughter "fragrant" and exactly fifteen months later to further narrow that down to a specific "Jasmine". Well, the two of us took on life and took it on the front foot. Both Shefali and Malati had decided that we will not to be the wallflowers of our female role model but rather the aggressive hunters of the male. We were sure of what we wanted, right from that first cigarette, and we were not shy of getting it.'

And there began a tale that held me riveted for the next hour. I have lived in Delhi since my late teens and lived independently, so, I knew of the 'modern' Delhi girls. But this first-hand account took me behind the silk—sometimes lace, sometimes cotton—curtains. Whoever spoke of the virtues of assertion, acquisition, achievement, control, decision-making, etc., as 'manly virtues' did not know what he was talking about. There is nothing gender specific about these…it is all a matter of confidence and social-standing. Malati was very candid about her life, a candour that was all the more refreshing for being strained through a sieve of mature intelligence and flavoured with an absolutely secure sense of self. There was no posturing here. No justification of youthful indiscretions, no airbrushing of anything; this was what we did, warts and all. And we did it because we wanted to. And we enjoyed doing it. She did not offer any salacious details, she was not trying to make this sound like some wild romp in a teenage fantasy; she was merely recounting some facts about her and her sister's lives.

'You see, sex itself is overrated, for the most part. And grossly underrated for many more. And virtue and sex have absolutely no relationship with each other. Sometimes, sex and love have even lesser to do with each other. The worst thing that we are all collectively guilty of is associating guilt with sex. And Shefali and I were clear that we were not going to be guilty now, we were not going to be guilty ever. That would be unethical. So, if we were not sure about what we were doing or we felt that somebody was going to get hurt by it, then, we never went ahead. But then, boys never feel any guilt, do they? And they never seem to get killingly hurt, at least at being turned down because that they seem to expect all the time. What they sometimes have difficulty in handling is being taken up on. Basically, all that the boys ever want to do is to do it. So, why make such a big song and dance about it? I know they felt then that we were convenient for them, but what they did not realize then, and what many of them stumbled upon later, was how convenient they were for us. You see, we wanted to sample all the types, to see which one would really suit us. So, the gym type, the intelligent type, the artistic type, the well-travelled type, the drunk type, the dopey type, the athletic type, the nerdy type; we actually kept notes. After all, life has to be sampled a bit before you sit down for a meal at the table, don't you think?

'But here I go, talking on and on about myself. You must have had some pretty interesting growing-up years too. Let's hear about them?'

Now, this is a moment of blind panic. At the stage of life when Shefali and Malati were getting off chauffeur-driven Mercedes cars and slipping into 'hunt' mode at the places she mentioned like 'Ghungroo' or 'My Kind of Place'—both five-star discotheques, by the way—my mother was making *roshogollas* in a steel handi to celebrate the fact that Tubluda had sent the money from the US to buy the inverter that would keep the lights on during the load-shedding power cuts so that I could concentrate hard and study undisturbed for my *Uchho Maddhyomik*—board examinations. While the sisters were ticking off and moving down their lists of 'types', I, along with five other oily-haired boys of similar age, was standing around Budoda, our *Para'r Kewda* (the locality wastrel), who, with due ceremony, would produce from his pockets six precious heavily folded yet coloured pages of a five-year-old *Penthouse* magazine. In college, our idea of a sinfully good time in the hostel was drinking Old Monk rum and watching the blue films that our Bihari hostel president would play on the common room's VHS player. The closest we got to actual female flesh, in the flesh so to speak, was when we would sit next to some female classmate in a lecture hall. My comparing this to the Malhotra sisters' doings and their evolved learning would be like comparing a baby's first steps to an Olympic sprint… Ridiculous. I have to change the subject.

'My growing up years? Boring, boring… Really quite boring. I think I was born pretty much grown-up. But tell me something, how did you get the marks you must have gotten? I mean, not everybody makes it to the academic profession after all that… you know…'

'Ah, there you go again. The confusions of middle-class morals. You are now confusing sex with scholarship. What has one got to do with the other? We were focused on what we did. So, equally, we were focused on our studies too. Besides, you forget, I was studying literature in college and I had my Mummy at home. Literature is literature, whatever the language. My mother, from a very early age, had awakened a sense of poetry, drama, and really, a love of reading in me. Doing well in college was not an issue. Shefali too was a star student. In fact, she went on to do even better after her Delhi University graduation… Dean's List at Cornell and a PhD from Harvard. Let me explain this a little further. Shef and I had similar, almost exactly the same, data points from our 'encounters' with the 'nerdy type' and 'engineer type' boys that were separated over four weeks. According to both our data sources, the average IIT guy masturbates twice a day. Now, take that over twenty days. That's forty times.

'Now, calculate the time, sourcing of stimulatory material, effort, mental space, physical seclusion and all that this demands. Isn't it better to simply fuck your brains out with someone every twenty days at least? A lot more return for a little larger investment. Not that I'm knocking out masturbation—that has its points—but that's a different debate. This way, you have a lot of time left over for your academics or whatever you want to do since the issue of sex is dealt with, done and dusted, and can be easily addressed when the need arises again. You know, it does not stay on your mind then, hovering around and getting in the way of everything else that you want to do. Of course, you have to be ready to be called a slut but Shef and I were cool about that. After all, isn't it bumper-sticker wisdom that a slut is a woman with the morals of a man? There, there… you're looking shocked. I think we had that happening with a lot of the guys, that's why, I don't remember us being called sluts easily. And of course, we were discreet.'

Now, this was a gem of bumper-sticker wisdom that I was definitely not familiar with. And moreover, any woman with the morals of the kind of man that I was would probably be called a nun. Where was all this wisdom during my university days? How cruelly had I been deprived of this kind of knowledge? How was it that I, and I am certain all of my friends, never met this kind of person in college? What was it about the new caste system of New Delhi that prevented the free mingling of people like us and people like them? Well, we are mingling now, so, perhaps I should not be complaining. However, I cannot help but wonder about the ghosts of the residents-past of this very home, now restaurant. The eyes that are watching from behind the poster of a Beer that's 'Been Helping Ugly People Have Sex Since 1862', the ears that are listening to our conversation over the Billy Joel track that has now replaced Dire Straits. I cannot help but wonder what they make of Malati and Shefali. I wonder if they cluck their tongues disapprovingly behind their burqas, or whether they clap their hennaed hands in admiration, shouting out their version of 'You Go Girl!' and 'Wish I was you!' Perhaps, in this place of so much history, a new history is being made. Yes indeed, the sun is shining bright. It is, in fact, chasing away the shadows from corners that have, for far too long, been shrouded in darkness. It is lighting up the world in the way that only a tropical noonday sun in its prime can. I wonder though—how many people will get sunstroke? And how many people will be able to take this heat?

Day 169

'AND NOW, LADIES and gentlemen, may we invite your attention to the sparklingly clear, twice-treated water of our organically-filtered swimming pool. Come one, come all, line up for a dip into this source of health and well-being. Bathe yourself in its life-giving coolness. This is the pool of pools, the guarantee of happiness and health. Oh! I am so sorry, I made a little mistake, and this is the pool of fools! However, you sir, the fool of fools, my Fool No.1, you are welcome to it.'

'Stop being such a drama queen, Roshni. Shut up and stop it. That security guard is going to chase us off now. How dare you blame me? It was a joint decision. Both of us had decided that this was going to be our home, you are as much a party to this as I am and we have to be together to handle these challenges. And by the way, what's happened to you? Why are you behaving like this? Just what has gotten into you lately?'

'Well, you certainly have not, have you now, Mr He-Man? You handle this mess, I am out of here. Car keys, please.'

With that, Roshni stomps off, pushes aside the security guard who by now has reached us and marches off to the car park. I am left standing under the stilts of the columns that will one day bear the weight of our dreams and looking into the pools of filthy water that have gathered underneath.

The long awaited Delhi monsoon is now firmly upon us.

The clichéd image of a life-giving rain gently reviving a scorched earth is laughably far from the truth. The rain is a malevolent, pelting downpour. There is nothing gentle about the hissing, spitting skies now. Only the volume of the growling, thundering air matches the physical fury of the rain. It has always been all about power here—if Round 1 belonged to Hammer Heat, then the winner of this round is Water Cannon. The climate of the National Capital Region, like everything else in it, can easily be likened to a Worldwide Wrestling Championship. And that's also what the last few weeks of our marriage has been like—a Worldwide Wrestling Championship.

Roshni and I fought all the way to this current 'site visit'. This trek has become like some holy pilgrimage—the revered 'tirth yatra' of our Hindu tradition—with all its attendant discomforts and inconveniences. After my somewhat hasty accusations, FatBum and his son have not been part of our journeys; instead Roshni and I have taken turns driving up to the site. Today started off with some minor bickering that quickly degenerated into intractable position-taking. 'Why can't you see there's a pothole ahead? I mean you do have eyes, even if you wear spectacles' quickly became 'Since my driving skills are so manifestly subpar, why don't you drive?' This statement was followed by a two-minute silence with the ignition off and the car pulled over to the side of a shallow yet gushing brown river which by the way was what the road had become and it was in this 'river-road' that I had lost the pothole that was so very visible to my lynx-eyed wife. The rain drumming off the roof of the Alto was the only accompaniment to the very voluble silence within it. Finally, Roshni, ever the practical one, was the one to break it, 'Look, we have a job to do, just let's go ahead and do it. If you like and if you insist on always being so contrary, then move over and indeed, I will drive.'

Obviously, my masculine pride would not hear of this, so I hunched over the seat, cleaned my much-maligned spectacles, moved closer to the windshield and once more plunged into the river.

Why would they do this? By what earthly leap of logic could they begin constructing new drains—and with their proven civil engineering excellence, thus block off all the old ones with the mud and the construction debris of the new—just three weeks before the monsoons? Just so that all the rainwater could be channelled straight on to the newly surfaced roads? To create the potholes for me to drive into? And jeopardize my relationship with my wife? Not possible. There has to be a reason less perverse than this, less individually malignant and more generally harmful. There has to be some wisdom, some logic here that, perhaps, I do not understand.

While I was wrestling with these doctoral thesis-worthy leaps of logic and concentrating on sometimes driving and sometimes kayaking on the somewhere road and somewhere river, I was dimly conscious of Roshni talking of my college. She was enquiring about the reopening date and how the teachers, my colleagues, were spending their holidays. Confident that I was on safe ground here, I was answering calmly, 'College starts on Monday, next week. Most of us have been preparing for the new term. Some have been on holiday.' There was a short period of silence after this. And just when I was feeling that sublime, mystical, man-machine road-river oneness and picturing myself as the winner in a 'Need for Speed' video game—just when the intensity of my concentration was such that I was actually discerning potholes by the ripples on the water's surface and my Schumacher kind of reflexes were so finely tuned that I was manoeuvring the Alto with the smoothness of an F1 driver—that a firefight erupted from the passenger side.

'I wonder why you never tried any other career option. I mean it can't be healthy, doing the same thing over and over again. Nothing ever actually changes except the students. The staffroom, the courses, they all remain. Even your teachers, your colleagues, all always remain the same. That can't be healthy, you know. It's too much closeness, too much sameness.'

I was trying to comprehend the scale and direction of this attack—indeed, also its objective—while simultaneously trying to marshal resources to defend and counterattack when suddenly the battlefield changed. 'Why are we even building this house is really a mystery to me. And that too, in such a dump. Why? What is it ultimately going to be? Do you even realize or understand what makes a home, a home? I doubt it. Only thing you are thinking of is a house. Try and appreciate the difference, or there is no bigger fool than you.'

Dumbfounded by this new line of offence, I could only mechanically park the car, open the door and hold out the umbrella for Roshni, for we had now fought our way to Glenmont Greens. With an umbrella on top and a cocoon of injured silence all around, we, the married couple, made our way to the foundation of our dream—our nest, our very own home. Yes, the news was right, the foundations had been laid, the underground parking lots were ready and the building had bravely risen to a level above the ground. However, the builder, following the noble example of every kind of civil and urban architecture in this place, had wisely not catered for expensive frills like drainage. As a result, the whole area resembled nothing as much as a shallow pool large enough for some exotic marine mammal. And it was poised on the side of this green and scum-specked surface that Roshni made her rousing peroration, issued her invitation to a refreshing dip and then stomped off, shoving aside a somewhat bewildered security guard...

And for the record, leaving behind a more than somewhat bewildered husband. This is not the Roshni I knew. Obviously, something is troubling her, something more than just her underachieving husband of ten years, the one she is used to and has adjusted with. Or maybe it is only that I think so. Perhaps, the accumulated frustrations of ten years are now finally boiling over with the added heat of the growing awareness of a poor decision? Maybe she too is feeling a rising panic at where we have chosen to invest our life's savings and our lives' dreams? Maybe she too is having her doubts about the sanity of Gurgaon's town planners? Maybe she too is realizing that this city is modelled on a future that is beyond us, that this is a city plan that seems to be some Hollywood writer's vision of a post-apocalyptic urban settlement. After all, there are enough movies like this now. Maybe this is the Unplanned Urban Centre 2.0 or UUC 2. And we are mere fools that have voluntarily chosen to sink our monies and our dreams into this. Maybe, this is the realization that is gnawing away at her too and maybe that is why she is behaving like this? A moment's thought on this and the rejoinder pops up—no professor, no. I am sorry to sound flippant, but that theory does not hold water.

While talking to myself and revelling in the delicious irony of my theories not holding water while my shoes and clothing are definitely holding it, I have waded my way to the car park and because the pouring rain has made a mockery of the umbrella, I have rolled it up and am using it to jab my way forward, just so that I do not tumble into any water-camouflaged pothole. The car park is an outsize square of raised concrete with a blacktop cover that is triumphantly holding its own against the rising waters. It is like a huge black square island with exactly symmetrical car-sized white lines painted on it that stands unsubmerged in proud defiance of the chaos all around it. It looks like a sort of last bastion of professional order and good design in the midst of the frothing confusion that surrounds it. On it are ranged series upon series of cars awaiting their owners—all comfortable and dry inside—while the machine-gun-like raindrops ricochet off their impenetrable metal hides. I am looking forward to the dry towel and the change of clothes that I had thoughtfully put in a plastic bag on the rear seat of the Alto.

Range Rovers, Fortuners, Audis, BMWs, Mercedes—they're all here; Gurgaon's show of strength is on full display and the car park is the show window of achievement. Even a humble Corolla and a humbler Swift are sometimes spotted but alas, there is no sign of my humblest Alto. I search high and low, and not just where we were parked, but there is in fact not a single Alto in the entire car park. While I am loath to accept it, I cannot help but face the fact that when Roshni demanded the car keys from me, it was not to wait in the car and let her rage subside. It was to leave, to exit the scene. What was it that she had said? 'I'm out of here'. Well, she seems to be well and truly out of here and this finality of exit—leaving me quite literally marooned—is yet another first in our relationship.

But why? If Roshni's previous irritations and anger were up for debate, this precipitate action is beyond any sort of debate— this is certainly not Roshni. This is not the smiling, ever-caring companion who would always remember to pack a sandwich for me and remind me via SMS when it was time to have my digestive medicines. In fact, that had become a bit of a joke in the staffroom and was called Roshni's bell. Even through my wounded pride and offended ego, I can see that merely the prospect of our dreams turning sour will not cause her to turn against me like this. There has to be something more here. This is personal. This rage is not against the rain, the discomfort, the dissolving roads and the dismal surroundings. This rage is against her Embee.

Travelling in a 'share auto'—one of Gurgaon's solutions to the problem of the complete absence of public transport—sandwiched between a man with an obvious fondness for radish matched with an equally obvious unreliability of the digestive process and a bunch of oversized schoolboys whose hobby seemed to be reaching out of the moving vehicle and lightly tapping the heads of every passing cyclist, I try to bring some calm sanity to my situation while the autorickshaw impudently dares the much bigger vehicles on the road with a show of speed and recklessness that is rarely seen outside of professional racing circuits. By the time I have gotten off at the metro station to take a train back home and registered that I am alive and well, albeit shaken, stirred, soaking wet and a trifle malodorous (after all, the radish assault lingers), a decision has been arrived at. I take my cell phone out of the plastic bag in which it was wrapped-up all this while and send Roshni a message: 'Cming home in metro. Vry disappointed with yr behaviour'. Before the phone can be returned to the dry and protective covering of the plastic bag, pat comes the return message: 'Y bother? Ynot go to Khan Market and hv a few beers?'

I can almost hear the penny drop. Suddenly, everything has a sharp, painful clarity. Each one of Roshni's seemingly unconnected statements now add up to a single agonizing point. I can see my reflection in the little puddle that has formed on the floor of the train from my dripping clothes and it vibrates, ripples and breaks up as the train thunders on towards my vibrating and rippling home. How does she know? How much does she know? Who has told her? Has she ever met Malati socially? Does she know that she is my colleague? Why is it that I do not remember? The train enters Delhi and from being a surface train with natural light and the occasional flashes of greenery that light up and add a chromatic variety to the interiors, it now plunges into subterranean depths and an unrelieved blackness rules outside. Is my life too going to be lit up only by artifice now? Otherwise, will it also plunge into unrelieved blackness?

Day 190

'I THINK WE should do a re-enactment of "Quit India".'

'Why not a reading of Nehru's "Tryst with Destiny" speech.'

'Sir, I think we should do a recitation of "Into that heaven of Freedom my Father, let my country awake" set to a video in which all of us feature.'

'What's with you guys? We should do something contemporary. I mean we've been free for longer than two, three generations now. Why this hang-up with the all this pre-independence stuff. Get modern, man.'

I can't believe what I've let myself in for. College has been open for two weeks now and I am sitting in on the third meeting of the 'Independence Day Celebrations' as a member of the Arts Council of the college. Three meetings and we have not yet decided what to do. Just how are we going to do what we decide to do after having finally decided what to do is another and perhaps longer story. I cannot believe that I invented this trap for myself and then let it close around me. When I started this, it seemed an inspirational stroke of genius, a master stroke of mendacity, the brightly shining key out of a relationship issue that was enfolding me in its foetid coils. Little did I imagine that a scant fortnight later, I would be closeted in a swelteringly hot room with a bunch of overeager students and some other unfortunate teachers trying to figure our way out of a problem of my desperate invention.

'Roshni, Malati and I are members of the college's Arts Council. Humanities Faculty Members have to have a representation on it. We were just discussing what to do for our Independence Day Celebrations since there would be no time after college reopens because the first few weeks are really busy. That's why we were meeting before, that's all there is to it. There is nothing more, nothing less. I don't know what spin has been put on it by whoever has told you but our meeting was professional.'

I just hate lying. Not for any highfalutin moral purpose but simply because I am so bad at it. When I lie, I sound and look even more like the bumbling fool than I normally come across as. This Arts-Council-and-Independence-Day-Celebration nonsense was the strategy I had dreamt up and revised many times over before entering home after that fateful SMS exchange. At that time, it truly seemed an inspirational stroke of genius because I knew that I could easily make it happen and that the lie of today could well become the truth of tomorrow. Therefore, lying today would become that much more easy and believable. Or so I thought. I don't think Roshni believed too much of it. She seemed resigned, strangely withdrawn. She seemed to know that some sort of excuse or explanation would be forthcoming, something bordering on plausible, something that I could believe in and therefore would be glib about. She seemed to be somehow expecting this.

Of course, she has had more time than me to think this through and it did sound pretty obvious and straightforward; after all, a very good reason for two colleagues to meet is work. So, maybe this is what she was expecting. But this acceptance, this tired welcome of a trite solution that came just too pat, is what has me worried much more than her screaming or ranting. Would not an honest, legitimate anger be preferred? Why didn't she ask me why I never told her of this meeting or never told her anything of Malati at all before this? If it was all so innocent and professional, how is it that it was never shared with her? After all, we do talk to each other about each other's work and we do discuss each other's co-workers. Well, to put it correctly, we used to.

At least, the other mystery is solved. The mystery of who ratted on good old Embee quaffing beers in a lonely hearts restaurant with a fiery hot bombshell is no longer a secret— it was the muscle-bound Rocky. Though why he should be following me around and reporting on my movements is another mystery. Or was it that he just so happened to be there with his friends? Chilling out on an afternoon? At bit unlikely because Khan Market is not really the place for young, first-year college crowd, or so I think. So, what was he doing there then?

'Sir, I am telling you we should be doing a video. It'll be great fun and you should have some fun sometimes with your students. You're always so serious.'

Wearing blue jeans, a tight mauve DKNY sleeveless T-shirt, with a mass of curls on her head and some residual pimples of adolescence on her cheeks, this girl is holding up some puerile script that she has written, as she is proud to announce 'proactively', and is looking at me expectantly now. Behind her, I can see the laughter in Malati's eyes, my fellow 'Arts Council' member. She mouths 'have fun' silently at me and drops one of her eyelids in a lazy wink. Were it not so absolutely preposterous, I could swear that this residually-pimply girl was actually flirting with me—'have some fun sometimes with your students' indeed. Maybe she was proactive about arts more than mere scriptwriting.

'Yes, I think we really should have some fun. So, let's do

everything. Why just a recitation, a dramatic rendering, a visual montage or a film? Mr Sharma, our principal, has great hopes of this Arts Council which I convinced him to institute at the beginning of this term. So, let's not let him down. I propose we create a multimedia, multisensory, multidimensional project that has independence as its core thought.'

Desperation and frustration are the triggers of this burst of inspiration and it is too late that I remember that these triggers have, in the recent past, not yielded reliable results. However, as I said, it is too late and unimportant enough to not think too much about it.

'What an idea, sirji,' says Ms Proactive Pimples. 'Orgasmic man, Coolly Orgasmic,' utters a Jesus-bearded, Fabindia kurta, jeans and chappals-wearing third-year Philosophy student.

I understood this to mean enthusiastic acceptance of the way forward, even if such was the academic richness and poetic fertility of the students here that this enthusiasm was compelled to be expressed through an overused advertising jingle or a reheated two-generation stale mish-mash of American university slang. But stop, why am I being so pompous again? I wish Roshni was here to prick that balloon. What have these expressions got to do with academic penury or poetic barrenness? Are they not simply just one more example of the mutations of the colonial fallout? As a student of history, one is familiar with the economic, cultural and historical consequences of colonialism. As a student of human nature, one sees it everywhere, especially in the deracinated, always insecure, laughably under-confident and frankly inadequate expressions that all of us use all the time.

None of us are native speakers of English. My mother tongue is Bengali and even if I do not know what languages Ms Pimple's or Jesus-Beard's mothers spoke in, I can almost guarantee that it was not English. Yet, the massive load of a language, its cultural baggage and its ability to allocate positions within the tribe, must be borne in all our cases by English. Naturally, we would resort to the shorthand of the advertising lexicon or its almost equally shallow equivalent, American university slang. And then, because our deepest thoughts can only be expressed by a language that is uniquely and individually our own—in my case a mix of Bengali, English and nowadays a lot of Hindi—a language that will never truly be understood by any other Indian or anyone else for that matter, because their mix and its proportions of constituent languages will always be different, we will ultimately stop thinking deep thoughts. All of us will speak in a strangely mutated, chopped-up patois whose native root has long been lopped-off and whose nourishing juices are now drying up. It will be a brutalized amalgam of tongues—a sterile hybrid. Language will only be used to exchange information and will have all the grace and poetic elegance of the binary code. And we will all have the capacity of the binary code for independent and deep thought which, of course, is exactly zero. But hey! It'll all be cool, orgasmically cool. Or was it coolly orgasmic?

'Thinking deep thoughts, Mr B? Or still worried? That was a smart move, by the way. Got them thinking and got them out of our hair. Now Dr Pasricha is helping them put the event together—they're already calling it a multimedia extravaganza, a multisensory look at the meaning of independence. Some of the students are confident of getting corporate funding from their fathers, uncles, etc. You're famous, Mr B. Of course, they'll need your famous "cell phone dictated notes" and by the way, that is something I too am truly impressed by. It is really an innovation and you are a creative type. But in this case, my dear creative type, in the case of the multimedia multisensory look at the meaning of independence, I think Dr Pasricha will get the credit. As usual, you seem worried. Can I help you with a coffee? Relax, here only, in the staffroom. I am not asking you to brave Khan Market again.'

I have of course told Malati all about Roshni's knowledge of our trysts. It was with her that I fleshed out the deception plan and approached our principal, Mr Sharma, to moot the idea of an Arts Council whose first product would be the Independence Day Celebration—a 'first time for our college, sir', 'tomorrows SRKs and Amitabh Bachhans could be from here sir'—and all that. After this, Malati and I are, well we can't be called brothers-in-arms, maybe 'not yet lovers-in-arms' in this whole mess.

'Was he there alone? That's the question that you need to ask. We both know that there are better places than Khan Market for a 20-year-old to hang out in. The question to be asked is, actually, there are two: a) was he following you? In which case, there's a logical reason for him to be there; and b) was he there with someone who might have more of a fondness for Khan Market than he does.'

I have told Malati nothing of either my suspicions or of my premature articulations regarding Roshni and Rocky. Yet, with the unerring instinct of someone who is far more experienced than I am in these matters, she is asking all the right, at least all the uncomfortable, questions. I had got as far as 'what was Rocky doing there?' She has gone further 'who might he have been with?'

'And Mr B, once again, I am asking you this, why do you continue with this hangdog look? What is the matter with you? What have you gone and done that should cause you any guilt? You just had a couple of coffees and beers with me, that's all. I am sure that much is allowed in your marital relationship. But here you are, mooning about it the whole day like you've committed some sort of mortal sin. Grow up a bit, will you?

Whatever in the world is going to happen to you if we were to really have an affair?'

With that, she places a cup of coffee on the table in front of me and takes her seat opposite. I am sure it was no accident that as she leaned over to place the coffee and sugar in front of me, her right breast squashed with calm resolve against my shoulder.

'But I don't think we ever will, so let's not even go there.'

I can only feel a hot and heavy spot on my shoulder where her breast has so recently been and a warm flush mounting my neck and face. 'And pray why, Malati? Why should you be so categorical about an affair between us never happening?'

'It's very simple, don't you see? I am a married woman.' And then, she busies herself with answering messages on her phone.

'Why are you looking so dumbstruck, Mr B. Oh, I see! It's again the confusion of your morality system, isn't it? First, you associate morality with sex and then you dissociate it from a relationship, isn't that it? Happy healthy sex is immoral but if you can achieve that, then having sex outside of your relationship is moral, is that it?? Here is a woman who has had no qualms about having sex earlier, so what's changed now? That's about it, isn't it? Perhaps it's not as simple as that, Mr B. Perhaps, it's not simple at all.'

'Actually, I never made such a mathematical correlation Malati. In fact, I am full of admiration for your guts and your clarity. I wish I could be, uh, could have been like that, I mean. And I am certainly not suggesting that we jump into bed. My curiosity was intellectual, as to why you were so categorical about dismissing the possibility. It was certainly not biased by what you have shared with me earlier. Maybe I thought that you do not find me an attractive enough participant in these games.'

'Interestinger and interestinger, Mr B. But alas, I am no Alice and this is no wonderland.'

As she finishes her coffee and leaves, I think that while I never had too much, and certainly never the correct, idea of what women were ever talking about, this was a whole new language. Malati had taken it to a different level. Forget about my not understanding it, this was not even English. Maybe this is another of those mutations of the colonial fallout I was ruminating on earlier.

'A multimedia extravaganza', 'a multisensory look at the meaning of independence'—the show should turn out quite well I should think. This is the ground that I am sure of. If there is one thing that has been my most faithful lover, that one thing has been my love for the subject I teach. Honestly, I don't know whether I love teaching, but I certainly do love the study of history. And simply because I love it so very much, some of it does rub off on the students. Here they are... All happily engaged in creating a project on what otherwise would have seemed like a dull and boring subject. Something that has been drummed into heads ever since primary school is now becoming alive and real to them. Perhaps, I don't understand Malati's language, but my students will certainly understand the kind of history that I will teach them.

Day 211

SOMETIMES, LIKE NOW, soaked and scrubbed by a month and more of unrelenting rains, the Delhi-that-could-have-been emerges briefly from the Delhi-that-is. The skies are washed clean, cerulean blue. The temperatures are a rain-bookended bearable, indeed pleasant 24 to 28 degrees. The fragrance is of moist earth. The roads are empty because it is the middle of the day on a public holiday and mine is one of the few cars on these wide, open avenues of an imperial city. The fact that this is also one of the greenest metropolises on the planet is apparent. An intolerably small-minded racist he might have been, but Lutyens certainly had the right idea when it came to conveying grandeur... Broad streets radiating out of a central circle with huge, slow-growing and shade-providing trees on either side and impressive manors set on acres of grounds. This is truly envisioned as a capital city. I have left the tombs of the Lodi's and their gardens behind and have been transferred from the fifteenth century to the twenty-first. Driving away from what used to be the village of Malcha before it was appropriated by a stroke of the imperial pen for the grand city of New Delhi and its villagers summarily banished to dusty Sonipat in Haryana, I move into diplomatic territory. Shanti Path, the Road of Peace, neatly bisects acres of green lawns with embassies, high commissions and foreign missions on either side. Straight as an arrow, it shoots southward towards Moti Bagh, the Pearl Garden, home to some of the more senior bureaucrats of the country. USA, Britain, Australia, Canada, France, Japan, Germany, Poland, even Pakistan—all flit past my lowered window like sped-up images in a slideshow. This drive is truly serving its purpose. It is calming me down, settling my mind. Shanti Path is indeed the Road to Peace for me.

I have left behind a home that is a seething cauldron. Into the already volatile combination of Roshni and myself, now has been added the incendiary compound of Tubluda. Plus, the fact that the construction of our new home has stopped and knowing the reason why the builder is refusing to take calls or answer emails is adding the spark to this dry and combustible tinder. I once read somewhere 'there are no coincidences, there are only conspiracies' and 'it's not that you're paranoid, they're actually out to get you'. Increasingly, both of these statements seem to be true. Why in the world should Tubluda, the jet-setting entrepreneur come to India twice in six months and then choose to do something that he has never done before— desert his beloved CR Park and shack up with his not-so-beloved younger brother? Why should the builder, after having smoothly reached up to the first floor, suddenly stop all construction? It cannot be just because he has not received the 'External Development Charge' from the allottee of Unit No. GG1C1114? More than anything else, why should my wife of ten years, my ever-smiling, joking, caring Roshni turn so snappy and irritable with me?

Parking my car at the Rail Museum at the end of Chanakyapuri and the beginning of Moti Bagh, I climb down to one of Delhi's hidden treasures, the Ring Railway. This started off with the ambitious hope of solving the city's urban transit issues, but, unfortunately, shared the same glorious disdain of having any connect with practicality that all such solutions in this city seem to delight in, and has, over the years, fallen into disuse as a passenger transit solution. I am told that it is sometimes used as a rail freight corridor. Thankfully, this is not one of those times and I get the solitude that I so desire. Walking along two gleaming rails in a steep cut in the urban landscape—a cut that has been transformed by the monsoon rains into a riotously green valley—while the cacophony of the city rages overhead, is indeed a thought-provoking experience. Here again, I marvel at the triumph of strength that this city epitomizes. This is no calming green vista. It is a jungle where every green shoot of life is locked in mortal combat with the other for the last drop of moisture, for the last ray of the sun. The conqueror of the largest area is a thorny shrub. Amongst these, somewhat incongruously, bloom bright flowers throwing splashes of colour and perfume amongst the thorns and the scrubs. By the end of my perambulations, I need to decide whether I am going to be the flower or the thorn. 'Going' is perhaps too ambitious a participle, 'deciding' too hopeful a verb, both implying, as they do, a sharp individual choice. Maybe, a more honest ambition would be a simple recognition—to know whether I am the flower or the thorn or maybe even the green shoot transformed to a brown twig, choked and asphyxiated more by its own aspirations rather than simply the competition.

Ten days ago, I walked in on Rocky and Roshni. No, scratch that—that sounds like a scene from a Vivid Entertainment Production. I *found* Rocky at home with Roshni. Heavy rains had resulted in classes being cancelled and coming home just after noon, I let myself in with my own set of keys. Putting away my umbrella and books, I walked into the kitchen to brew myself a cup of tea only to find Roshni atop a step-ladder picking up a pickle jar from the top shelf with Rocky crouched at the bottom holding both legs of the ladder tightly. Sounds of laughter were ebbing away as I entered unannounced. It was a scene of happy domesticity, the likes of which I had not seen in our home for a long while. My entrance was the only discordant note in this Indian Norman Rockwell scene and Roshni was startled enough to drop the pickle jar. Of course, Rocky, the star athlete that he is, made no mistake and scooped it up like the ace cricketer Jonty Rhodes before it hit the floor. And, there we were—me, a middle-aged man wearing a khadi shirt, jeans and leather sandals looking at his wife through his rain-misted spectacles, his jeans, T-shirt and apron-wearing wife looking down at him from the third rung of a ladder, and a spectacularly muscled young hunk looking up at the both of us with a pickle jar in his hand.

'Back early?' was the statement of fact delivered in a flat monotone by Roshni who, naturally, was the first one to recover. 'Back early' was my reflexive affirmative. The next contributor to this sparkling feast of reason and flow of soul was none other than the muscle-bound Rocky. Placing the pickle jar on the shelf and dusting off the seat of his jeans, he turned to Roshni and said, 'I'm off then. Please tell uncleji for this evening.' With a mumbled 'Bye Uncle' to me, he ducked his head under the kitchen door lintel and ran downstairs to the Khanna home. By now of course, I was looking askance at Roshni and couldn't help but snap out a curt, certainly more curt than I intended, 'So, what's happening?' The 'here' in the question was left unsaid, but was clearly implied. 'What is happening is that,' Roshni slowly and patiently explained in simple words like one would with a five-year-old, 'Mr Khanna has some new information about our investment and is coming up in the evening to share it. Also, since you are more worried about the pickle, Mrs Khanna is sending some of her famous gobi paranthas up with Mr Khanna and I thought my mother's mixed veg pickle would go very nicely with it, so, I asked Rocky to help me bring it down from the shelf…' She took off her apron, hung it on the hook on the wall and as she walked past me in the doorway, tossing a 'not even five minutes ago' over her shoulder.

My thoughts? I do notice that FatBum has been promoted to Mr Khanna and also register the fact that he is coming to meet us in the evening. Also, our new home has been demoted to 'investment' and Rocky is certainly no longer 'that brain-dead Khanna son'.

At the same time, the image of the locked downstairs door pops into my mind—something I had noticed while walking up the stairs just now. This means that there was nobody in the Khanna household when Rocky was summoned to help and gratuitously timed at 'not even five minutes ago'. I do not brew any tea, but, I simply turn around and go to bed to sleep for the next three hours.

'Arre, it is a matter of three people you know…three people with three independent viewpoints, *haanji*. All are brothers and all are fighting with each other—what to do?'

It is evening and as promised, FatBum has ascended to our home and we are in the midst of doing justice to his wife's gobi paranthas and my mother-in-law's mixed veg pickles. A pot of curd has also made its way to the table as have many cups of hot sweet tea. After a long time, our home is feeling like it used to. Mr Khanna, with his extra weight and his earthy wisdom, has brought in a lightness to our flat and into our lives. Roshni has even served me my trademark Lipton with extra sugar and two Marie Lites before I start on the paranthas. The conversation has so far been on light and easy subjects, a warm-up to the main topic which has just been broached.

So far, I have only been experiencing FatBum and his effect, it is only now that I start concentrating on what he is saying and suddenly the import of his information starts to get through to me. I sit up and take note and notice that Roshni too is doing the same. Apparently, the plot of land on which Glenmont Greens is slowly and shakily rising was once the property of Chaudhary Hukam Singh Yadav. This Haryanvi Chaudhary had, as is the norm in gender-skewed rural Haryana, five sons and no daughters; of course, one does not dare to ask how or why only these XY chromosome-loaded guns fire with these super masculine people.

Out of this worthwhile brood, one was lost to a drug overdose and another fatally injured in a land dispute shootout which is, again, par for the course with this kind of landowning family in this part of the country. The three remaining sons were the inheritors of the land and sold one parcel to the developer of Glenmont Greens as he was a developer with eminent pedigree and impressive credentials standing tall in Gurgaon. All their other lands were sold to petrol pump franchises, warehouses, commercial and business enterprises, 'Government Authorized Drinking Places' and other such buyers who were of no interest to us. Interestingly, three half-acre plots had been retained for individual 'farmhouses'.

Even more interesting was the twist in the tale. After the passing away of the lamented Chaudhary Hukam Singh—sadly due to cirrhosis of the liver—there were suddenly not one, but three Chaudharys, each self-appointed. Naturally, in every argument, each was right—after all, each of them thought of himself as The Chaudhary—and therefore could not be wrong. Equally naturally, no share could be large enough for any one, it had to be all or nothing. And thus began the fight. All brothers, all fighting with each other...what to do?

All this was certainly interesting from an academic or

storytelling point of view. This was after all the story of the Mahabharata, the story of the Mughals, the story of every family of any standing in the subcontinent. It was a story that has been told over and over again for thousands of years, in family after family with various permutations and combinations while maintaining a singular thematic consistency. Jealousy, greed, the sure knowledge that the winner takes it all, call it what you will, is hardwired in the DNA of our species. It is in fact the cause of our evolutionary success. A very interesting topic, I am sure but, of what relevance to us? And this, shorn of the needless verbiage and intellectual contortions, was the question I posed to FatBum. In short, I asked him, 'Three brothers are fighting. So?'

'Arre, professor saab! You are not understanding! *Yeh to kanoon hai.* It is the law. Thirty per cent of the property is always in the hands of the original owners. This means that 30 per cent of your Glenmont Greens is in the hands of these three brothers. Now, they are fighting. Now, you know that *ijjat*, you know, prestige, is more important to them than anything else. So, one does not want the other to profit from it. It does not matter if they themselves earn nothing from it. You see, money is nothing to them, their only concern is that the other should not profit because it is a matter of *ijjat*. So, they have all told the builder that nothing further can happen. If the builder builds anymore they will create trouble for him.'

'Create trouble? But Khanna saab, this builder is no bachcha. He is a well-known builder of Gurgaon. I am sure that he is not scared of the trouble that these three brothers can create? He must be having his own muscle, *na*?' Roshni has jumped into the discussion with her own incontestable logic—strength must be matched with strength, a lesson that we learn from our cradles.

'Of course *beti*, of course. But, you see, he is a businessman. Number one, he does not want trouble, and number two, he cannot afford to have 60 per cent of his building empty.'

'60 per cent of his building is empty?'

'You see, the builder has sold only 40 per cent to people like you. That's when he begins construction. As the building goes up so do the prices and then he starts selling the other 30 per cent that he owns at higher and higher prices. It's simple, the price goes up with the building and he puts his own inventory in the market then…when the price is up.'

'So, what's stopping him now? Why is he not building?'

'The brothers will not let out their flats. They will not rent to anyone so that no one can rent from their brothers. And they will spread this news. So, not only will their 30 per cent remain empty, the builder's 30 per cent will also never get sold. This will become a *bhoot bangla,* you know, a haunted building. Some more of that pickle please…it is really very good. That's why he's not building any more, you see. He does not want to put any more money into it until the situation resolves. Common sense.'

Roshni and I catch each other's eyes over the sight of our bringer of bad tidings stuffing his face. It is not a pretty sight. The news he brings is even uglier. Our dreams are dying stillborn. Our hopes, no matter how soured they may have become since we launched on this enterprise, now seem to be foundering. For the first time in many months, Roshni and I are united in a common cause. I get up, walk around the table and stand behind her with my hands on her shoulders.

'So, what will happen now, Khanna saab?' Roshni asks for both of us.

'Happen? Nothing will happen, beti. These things happen. You will either have to wait it out which is what most people will also do because they are mostly investors, not end-users or you could unite and make things happen. But, don't worry, it will get sorted. Sooner or later, a reasonable solution will be found. But, you can never tell with these Haryanvi Jats, they are all *sarphira*. Then, there is always the law; the builder has a contract with you and he will have to honour that. Just check your builder-buyer agreement...is there any delay or penalty clause for the builder?'

Wiping the last of the pickle from the plate with the last of the parantha and downing the last of the tea, FatBum fires off his last salvo, 'But do you really want to go to court? As a single person, you will have a really tough time. What you should do is form an association of all the flat-owners and then go to court as a body. But then, first you have to find all the other flat owners. It is a difficult job. Maybe the Internet can help?'

'Khanna saab, once again, in your opinion, and you are the expert in these matters, what do you think is our best option?'

'Frankly, the best option is to wait it out. It could take years, but then, you are not paying anything more for it now. It is all construction-linked. Or if you want, I could perhaps fix a face-to-face with the builder. I do know the local police officers well and that meeting could be fixed. But I must tell you, this is a double-edged sword. Have you dealt with the police earlier? No? I thought so. Very dangerous, both their friendships and their enmities, very dangerous.'

The paranthas have finished and so, it seems, has our conversation. The cold hard reality of the situation is facing us. FatBum, for whatever his faults, has at least clarified matters for us. Now, even if we are uncomfortable with the knowledge, we know the reason for this sudden cessation of all work at the site. Maybe this will bring Roshni and me together again. Maybe this cloud will have a silver lining.

Seven days later who should drop in but Tubluda, Dr TwoBlue himself, for a global dental conference in Delhi itself. 'And, since I am here already, I thought I'll extend my stay for a week, ten days, and see how things are shaping up with my kid brother. I just thought it'll be nice to catch up with you guys, you know.' Tubluda is certainly not unwelcome; it is just that his visit is so completely unexpected and so entirely out of character. Each of his previous entries into India have been preceded by weeks of planning, sheaves of emails being exchanged, even excel sheets of schedules and invites to his 'get-togethers' being worked out. Yes, this time too we had exchanged emails, I knew of the conference, but he had never confirmed his attendance and I certainly had no idea that I would be opening the door one fine evening to the sight of Tubluda with his bags at my doorstep. 'Surprise, surprise! Just like the old days, eh, when we used to have guests dropping in without telephone calls. Ha! Hell, in those days we never even had phones either, did we?'

Surprise, spontaneity, this kind of forced gaiety—all these are qualities that one would never have associated with Tubluda. Roshni and I are both very surprised, but Roshni, God bless her soul, outdoes herself with her welcome. The guest room is spruced up and Tubluda is fixed up with a hot meal, a hot bath and clean sheets in a comfortable bed before he can surprise us any further with his new found garrulity.

'Just what is going on? How is it that I did not know of this? Did you call him over? Running to big brother to solve your problems, are you? And since you can't make your way there, you call him over? Is that it?' Arms akimbo, hair disarrayed, eyes blazing, nostrils flared, housecoat tightly knotted around the waist, this is a completely different Roshni from the warm, gentle, ministering angel who settled Tubluda into his bed, not five minutes ago, with calm assurances that we would talk at length the next day after his jet lag had worn off.

'I what?! Of course not? What are you talking about? Of course, I did not call him over. I did not even know of this visit? What has gotten into you? How can you speak like this, Roshni?'

'Of course, you would not know of this. That's too much of an ask, isn't it? To expect that you would really know something of what is happening in the real world. I wonder how much you really know of anything at all? Sometimes, I really ask myself what I am doing with you?'

Roshni's words of that evening three days ago are still resonating in my head. Yes, she is doing her 'duty' with Tubluda, making sure that all his creature comforts are taken care of, but I am still frozen out. I can't decide which is better—this silence or the hissing stabs that she lashed out with. At least with the latter, the boil is lanced, the pus released. The problem is with the scars that are left behind. I know I will neither forget nor ask that—'what is she doing with me at all' or 'how much do I really know about anything at all'. While all this is gnawing at my insides, there is no release. Tubluda's presence ensures that we maintain a civility amongst ourselves, but I can feel the strain. Sooner or later, something will have to give and I both dread and look forward to that moment. Do I really 'know nothing of what is happening in the real world?'

'*Oye dekh, ganja pi raha hai! Ek charsi mil gaya Hira Singh, aaj ka pehla* doper.'

Suddenly, two burly and pot-bellied men, both in Delhi Police uniform have materialized around me. Obviously, they were walking down from the other side of the bend in the track while I was sitting on a boulder smoking a thoughtful cigarette. They have just run into me, literally, a sitting duck. I get up to set the record straight—no, I am not smoking dope and I am no junkie, rather, I am a college professor. But before I can say much, actually even while I am in the process of saying it, one grabs me by the back of my neck, the other bends my hand over my wrist and both together force me to sit down again.

'Take it easy brother, I am no doper. At least, not anymore. I was just smoking a cigarette. I just wanted some alone time.'

'Oh yeah! Isn't that what they all say?'

'I wouldn't know what they all say. I can only talk about myself. I don't have your experience with criminals.'

'This is a smart one, Hira Singh. Got a mouth on himself, doesn't he?'

'Get your hands off me. You can't do this to me.'

'Shut your face, you swine! You're going to tell us what to do? You got it upside-down, we're going to tell you what we will do...to you.'

'Look, he's even got a little beard; maybe we can say he is the terrorist we've been warned about. In any case, let's plant some drugs on him.'

If we're lucky, we can really have some fun with this one.'

With this, one of these guys actually starts fumbling with my belt buckle. By now, I am beyond panic and start screaming loudly in English. That seems to slow them down a bit and they content themselves with cuffing me round the head a couple of times and abusing me in the vilest possible language. Between them, they frog march me up on to the road and to their waiting vehicle—a Maruti Gypsy fitted with an intercom—with a third cop waiting inside. This one is a grizzled veteran, a much older man wearing sergeant's stripes on his sleeves and he explains the situation to me. Apparently, there is a terrorist red alert in the city, therefore, all rail tracks are being patrolled and all loiterers being picked up. Loiterer? At my indignation, the older man simply laughs and then asks me to explain what I was doing if not loitering? Did I think that this was the classroom and lectures were going on? Was I saying thanks for the fact that, for once, I was receiving no backchat from the students? Heavy-handed witticisms abound and by now all three policemen are laughing. Red-faced and trying to reclaim the last remaining shreds of my dignity, I complain about the mistreatment I have received and mention social media. At once, the mood changes. All laughter stops. The sergeant seems to lose interest and flicks his head to his two underlings. The movement is choreographed—one reaches into my shirt pocket and drops a glassine envelope into it, the other bends me over the Gypsy bonnet and stretches both my hands behind my back. Suddenly, I am handcuffed with my hands behind my back, a most humiliating first-time sensation for me. 'Possession of drugs with intent to sell,' one of the policemen intones in Hindi. 'Smack, brown sugar and ganja found in his shirt pocket as well as pants' pockets,' pronounces the other while putting his hands into my pants pockets and placing one more plastic packet in each.

'Your next lecture is going to be to the magistrate, professor saab.'

'*Haan*, but before that, you are going to the lock-up to meet the rest of the faculty, oh Guruji. *Baaki staff se bhi miliye toh*. And I am sure that everyone in the lock-up will have a lot to learn from you, sir! *Acchi* introduction *hogi*.'

I had to hold my ears and say sorry to these bullies. I had to beg on bended knees to be let off. I had to write a letter of apology explaining my walk and mentioning my thanks to the helpful police officers who guided me back to my car after I fell down and lightly bruised my face on the rail track. The last thanks was because I had to suffer the further indignity of being clouted in the face when I began the letter in English. '*Oye*, we are not professors, write it in Hindi, you ass.' Of course, I had to pay up every last rupee I had in my wallet. And then, finally, I was gently lectured by the sergeant about how all this could have been avoided and how I really should wise up to the ways of the world. Of course, all this was for my own good and I would be a better man for this lesson. They were just upholding the responsibility of the police force, educating the common citizen about right and wrong.

The same excuse—the dreamy professor had fallen on the tracks—was made to Roshni and Tubluda when I went home and they saw me. I wonder if 'on' is the right preposition because, nowadays, I feel that I am increasingly falling 'off' the tracks.

Day 232

'IT'S THE BREATH of life, you know, or water of life. I mean, that's what it literally means. That's where the word came from, from the Irish or Gaelic language. Anyway, that's what it means and you're supposed to add just a dash of water to it. That's all. To release the flavour, that's it... You don't want to drown it now, do you?'

Tubluda has taken it upon himself to educate me on the fine art of whisky drinking. Blenders Pride, ice and water which was my staple at Aitbaar is now firmly off the list. A series of exotic single malts have been lined up and I am being coached in the nuances of the peaty, smoky Islay malts versus the full-flavoured smoothness of the Glenlivet. And, wonder of wonders, the owner of Aitbaar has joined us at the table for a toast of single malt and all these whiskies are from his private collection. 'Sir, I recognize a true-blue world-travelling gentleman when I see one and of course, I will have the right spirits for him!' Tubluda, quite naturally, wanted to go to 1911, the bar at The Imperial Hotel, a five-star hotel at Janpath with a serious Raj hangover, but, I persuaded him to wend his way to the much humbler Aitbaar. 'There are some things that I should be familiar with Tubluda, if not the prices or the tastes, at least the surroundings.' Finally, the owner's abject obsequiousness sealed it for Dr TwoBlue and here we were, swirling and tasting like seasoned global professionals, and gulping and swallowing like thirsty Indians. So far, the only question I have is why could not we have done this at home? Maybe Roshni too could have joined us?

There are many first times that mark this evening. It is the first time that Tubluda and I have gone out for a dedicated drinking session together. Oh sure, we have been having drinks together since I started working but that was always with meals or at parties with other people present. And always to show that we were not hidebound traditionalists, rather we were modern, academically solid, intellectually gifted, broad-minded Bengalis. This is the first time that Tubluda and I have gone out to 'talk, really talk' and that kind of talking, as the good doctor maintains, begins with drinking. I only hope that it does not end with puking because I know my own 'non true-blue world-travelling gentleman' capacity. It is also, almost certainly, the first time that so many single malts have graced an Aitbaar table.

'Ideally, one should smoke a cigar with this but I don't smoke at all now and there you go committing blasphemy with your Gold Flake.'

'C'mon Dada, it's just whisky, great whisky I am sure, but still, just whisky.'

Tubluda does not say anything. I think this shocking irreverence has robbed him of the power of speech. Persisting with my insensitivity, I compound the sacrilege by asking if I can add some more ice and water as this almost undiluted spirit is bringing tears to my eyes. I do not ask just to be needlessly and provocatively irreverent or to puncture Tubluda's balloon of sanctimonious obeisance to 'just' whisky, but because I actually want to keep a clear head. I am very interested in the 'talk' because I want to know just what has happened with Tubluda that he should be slumming it like this?

Tubluda adds some ice cubes and pours some water into my glass with a rueful shake of his head—'pearls to the swine' is the expression on his face—fortifies himself with an extra pour of the Laphroaig and then gets down to the serious business of the evening.

'You are facing some troubles, aren't you? I can see it on your face and the way you are behaving.'

My troubles? What is this? I thought this evening was going to be about him? How come he's bringing up my troubles?

'You can't hide it from your elder brother. I can see it. Actually, this sort of thing—this new flat and paying for it, all these stresses and tensions—does not suit you. You are an academic, you know, All this is not really for you, I can see you're cracking up. Now, take for example, me. I have been doing business for so many years. All this is very simple for me. Oh, yeah, it's like cakewalk, man.'

So many years in the US and Tubluda has still not lost the inflexions or the speech patterns of Indianized English learnt late in life. In it, the occasional 'Oh yeahs' and the 'cakewalks' sound incongruously funny. I am tempted to laugh but check myself in time. I must go easy with the liquor or this evening is going to be one long giggle.

'What tensions Dada, I am fine. Oh yes, a little extra money would be great but that's okay. And of course, if the flat was located in say, Singapore, that would have been even better but, I'm okay.'

'No, no, no, no. You are not seeing the future, *babu*. I admire your bravery but you are looking at a life sentence. How long do you think you will be paying off your loan for? And once you enter the flat, you are going to need another loan for the furniture, the fittings, etc. How are you going to pay that back? Your job will become the most important thing in your life and that will bind you down. It would prevent you from ever achieving anything else that you possibly could because you will not be able to afford to compromise the monthly salary as that'll be required for the instalments. So, you won't be able to risk leaving or losing your job. That will prevent you from doing anything else or even doing very well at this one because even to do very well at a job, one needs to take risks. And, you'll be running scared. This loan business is the burning of your wings buddy, the hobbling of your feet. This middle-class housing game in India is not liberation, it is enslavement. You enter the game and zap, you're sentenced for life. This game has been designed for investors and those with ready money to make more money. It's not designed to give you guys a home.'

I shift the whisky from one side of the glass to the other. Looking down and avoiding his eyes, I light another cigarette. Once again, Tubluda is asking difficult questions and I feel like I did thirty years ago—sweating in the *barandah* of our Behala house in Kolkata, scratching my head with the fingers of my right hand, while scraping the back of my left calf with the toes of the right foot as drops of sweat ran down the pencil marks of my algebra exercise book—Tubluda's a's and b's have once again disappeared into a confusing quicksand of 'a squares', 'b squares' and 2ab's. I know my answers to his sums are wrong. But like then, I still don't know what the right answers could be, or worse, how to get to them.

'I don't know about that, Dada. Lots of middle-class people like us are now buying homes at this stage. It's different for you guys, of course. You look at everything as an investment.'

'No, no. Not just that. You don't understand…your problems are just going to start with this. This is just the beginning, mark my words.'

It has always been like this with Tubluda. I guess it would

be the same between any two brothers separated by a large age gap growing up in what was still largely a traditional Bengali household. Any sentence from the elder to the younger would be prefaced with a 'No, no, you don't understand' and all homilies would conclude with a 'you mark my words'.

Carrying on with the tradition, the elder brother then launches into a lengthy—two pegs of whisky long—sermon on the perils of home-owning. Caesar might have said 'I came, I saw, I conquered'. Me? 'I smoked. I drank. I listened.' Finally—and I honestly think the whisky and the fact that he was talking to his commercially-challenged younger brother combined to make him confuse targets—Tubluda got to the point.

'Even for a guy like me it's very tough. That bloody CR Park house is keeping me up at nights now.'

Like most Indians of our generation, we were taught and have subsequently absorbed a very 'British' English, that is, a variety of English that was frozen in the subcontinent circa early twentieth century. The British may have forgotten the antiquated 'bloodys' and 'jolly goods' but I notice that these phrases have not shaken their hold over Tubluda's speech yet.

'You wouldn't believe what's happening. Ratna Pishi has got hold of a bloody lawyer and that bastard has gone ahead and sent me a letter. Bloody bastard! She is claiming the house!! For her own! She showed me some letter that Baba sent her ages ago and is now claiming that the house should, by rights, belong to her. Apparently, this was to be her Borda's gift to her and I am merely the instrument of that. What a mistake I made by not charging her any rent all these years.'

Tubluda is working himself into a foaming rage at the injustice of it all and has to calm himself down with another whisky. The next ten minutes are devoted to how one should never do favours to another, everything should be balanced, and with every give, there must be a take, otherwise, the balance is destroyed and the hand that is feeding is more often than not the one that is bitten.

'Somebody of course has been feeding her all this and poisoning her mind. Must be that lawyer, bloody swine! He doesn't know what he's bitten off, but he's finding out soon and getting a real shock in the process.'

I have no doubt about that. A seasoned businessman, my elder brother would, no doubt, have both defence and offence ready for this sneak attack. Little wonder then that he has parked himself in Delhi and certainly the reason why he is in my house and not at CR Park. As it transpires, he has declared total war. As the whisky flows, the story unfolds. A high powered battery of lawyers—attorneys and counselors as he calls them—have been unleashed upon the one misguided individual who had created and was representing Ratna Pishi's case. Even before the case hits India's convoluted legal machinery, this single simpleton has been inundated with paper and intimidated by the names on Tubluda's payroll. It is an unequal contest. Once the bugles have been blown, the battle has been joined. And since it is total war, Tubluda is showing no quarter and taking no prisoners.

'She's gotta go, man. She's just gotta go. She had a good thing going, she shouldn't have gotten above herself. Now, she's gotta go.'

'But, Dada, at this age and this stage, where is she going to go? She has absolutely no place left.'

'Then she shouldn't have shit her doorstep, should she? Did I ask her to lawyer up? Did I ask her to try to own what she was already getting for free? Man, you do charity and you get shit on. That's what happens, man, that's just what happens. She's going, man, and where she's gonna go is no business of either yours or mine.'

This is Tubluda, the businessman unmasked. This is the face that creates success, no, grabs it, in the cut and thrust of life. And Tubluda, for once, without saying it, is reminding me of how much I lack this face. I would never have been able to turf Ratna Pishi out and that's why, I, perhaps, will never own a home in CR Park.

'Why don't you move in there?'

Suddenly, I see a look of cold calculation in my older brother's eyes. All at once, I understand that I had prematurely arrived at what I thought was his point. There are more layers to this onion. His point was not only about himself and his troubles. Those he can sort out for himself. Why does he need me to drink whisky with him if he is going to only reclaim his property and turn his aged relatives out on the street? There is more here and I figure in that 'more'.

'See, it's perfect. You don't have to get into any of the hassles of home ownership for yourself. Nothing of all these stresses and tensions I was telling you of earlier. Of course, you pay me a monthly rental, but it will be nominal and I will write up the deed so that you can stay there as long as you like, maybe ten years, or maybe even fifteen. And in that time, you can save up all you like and finally buy your own home, cash down. That way you won't get hurt, you won't get caught in this vicious cycle of EMIs, unmade buildings, etc. You pay for what you see. Simple.'

However, to me, it is anything but that simple. I am a human being and not a calculating machine. Instinctively, I recoil against this idea. Somewhere, very deeply buried I am sure, but somewhere, there is something in me that wants to deserve what I get and I do not want to get something out of Tubluda's much reviled charity. Plus, of course, do I want to daily ask myself where Ratna Pishi is as I read a book in the drawing room or sleep in the bedroom?

Tubluda has an uncannily accurate reading of people and of situations. Maybe that's what makes him such a shrewd businessman. He looks at me, pats me affectionately on the back and says, 'Hey, no hurry, kiddo. You take your time. Talk it over with the wife. This night is for drinking between brothers. Get another one, brother!'

That night, after my incomplete if exhaustive whisky education, we stumbled home and I confided the details of Tubluda's offer and my trepidations about it to Roshni. Once again, we are in agreement. Roshni roundly rejects the mere thought of us being pawns on Tubluda's chessboard. 'Let him get his own tenants or leave the house empty as it was. In any case, asking Ratna Pishi to get out like this is just so cruel. So, she got misguided a bit, punish that greedy lawyer by all means but, how can you be so inconsiderate towards your own Pishi?' Whatever our differences might be and no matter how snappy Roshni seems to have become with me, it is moments like these that convince me that the fundamentals of our relationship are strong. There is a real meeting of minds between us, which I would be tragically foolish to overlook in the midst of all the distractions that we currently have.

'It's not just about being kind to Ratna Pishi, Embee. It's also about leading people on. He led Ratna Pishi to believe that this was her own house and that really changed her. It transformed her. And now, when he does not like the collateral effect of that transformation, he wants to beat her down to size. You remember my Baoji? He was nothing like that—at least he never blew hot and cold. He was uniformly judgemental. If he did anyone a favour, he would never let them forget it and remind them every waking moment that they were indebted to him, even his own daughters. My mother was never allowed to forget—even for a minute—that her life in that household was a favour granted to her by Baoji. That's why she never stopped cooking, cleaning, working, managing because, according to her, she was paying him back. Of course, it rubbed off on me too, it's strange to live your life repaying a favour.'

After what seems like ages, Roshni and I are lying in bed, holding hands and having a conversation like we used to. The room is in darkness, the air conditioner is gently whirring and Tubluda is snoring in the guest room.

'Neither of them seems to be a nice man to know, eh!'

'The world is not nice Embee. We both know that. Don't forget that both of them became and have become successful and well-respected people, pillars of society. You don't get there by just being nice, do you?'

The high, courtesy of the single malt, is wearing down. I can feel another sort of high coming on, 'So, where does one get by being nice then?'

'One gets to buy one's wife a home of her own. The kind her mother never had. The kind one's own aunt thought she had. A home where one and his wife can make a whole world for themselves.'

Tubluda left three days later. He was very gracious about our turning down of his proposal. 'Hey! Your call entirely. I was only trying to help.' Before leaving, he had a long chat with Ratna Pishi and got her to sign the various documents that his lawyers had drawn up. He chose not to share with us his final decision regarding her eviction or continued stay but he made it amply clear to all that this was his house and nobody should think otherwise.

The day after his departure, Roshni and I went to CR Park with a box of sweets to have tea with Ratna Pishi and talked about the years past and the years to come. She seemed a bit more teary than usual, but, on the whole, looked to have weathered this storm rather well. My personal opinion, which I shared gratis with Roshni, was that she has not fully understood either the implications of what she had done or the consequences that could have followed.

Meanwhile, our Arts Council has gained a certain notoriety in college. What started off as the fleshing out of an excuse to explain trysts in restaurants has now become a legitimate reason for Malati and I to spend an inordinate amount of time together. Our multisensory, multimedia extravaganza on Independence Day that was conceived of in a spur-of-the-moment act of desperation has become a huge hit. Ms Pimples and Jesus-beard—I still cannot remember their names—have been anointed 'Creative Directors'. Dr Pasricha, who, to his credit, displayed an unsuspected skill at managing the various talents that the students brought to the fore and guided the show to its flawless finale, has been receiving offers to script and choreograph more such shows from professional event management companies. Malati and I, supposedly the pair whose brainchild this Arts Council is, are daily invited to sit in on 'ideation' and 'brainstorming sessions'. In fact, my style of teaching, believe it or not, has a nickname in college—'Socrastic'. Apparently, like Socrates, I too ask questions of the students to elicit the point of the lesson, but can be aciduously sarcastic when faced with either ignorance or stupidity. The sarcastic Socrates's lectures have therefore been dubbed 'Socrastic'. I have been asked to deliver a series of lectures on the 1857 Revolt for which students have called in their friends from other colleges. The biggest lecture hall has been booked for the four-lecture series and it is touted, I am reliably told, on Facebook as the 'Socrastic Series'. My cell phone now requires to be recharged three times a day as I am recording more than my usual quota of lectures into it.

Life is suddenly very busy, unfortunately, the building site at Gurgaon is not. All construction at Glenmont Greens remains firmly suspended. While it is easy to gloss over my perturbation with this kind of breezy reportage, I am feeling the first fingers of a nameless dread tentatively probing my insides. What will happen if the building actually does not get made? Roshni and I have put everything that we had into this and our investment has not been just financial. All our calculations—considering the EMI to be the rental we would otherwise pay—were geared towards moving in by Diwali of next year, which is just a little more than a year from now. If we are unable to do that, we will be in all kinds of soups.

'There must be others like you. I mean, there can't be only investors who bought into this. There must be other end-users like you guys. You should really try and connect with them, at least to figure out some angles of what you could try to do now.'

It is late afternoon. Malati and I are sitting around a utilitarian faux wood table which is the unofficial 'Arts Council' meeting place in a staffroom that is still smelling of cauliflower, cabbage, pickles, roti, parantha and the other assorted ingredients of an Indian lunch. Most of the other staff have either left or are out for their post-lunch ambles. In front of us is spread out a student's proposition for a photography exhibition—'Yesterday's Delhi through Today's Eyes'. Though the title is clunky, the subject is very interesting and the student seems to be as creative as she is entrepreneurial. Her idea seems to be to shoot all of Delhi's monuments with a high-quality cell phone and she already has an 'in-principle' agreement with a new Chinese mobile phone company to sponsor the whole thing.

'How would I know how to contact them or even how to reach out to them?'

'That shouldn't be too difficult. See what this girl has done: First, she wrote a blog about her interest, then, she set up a Facebook page on Delhi's disappearing legacy and after getting hundreds of inputs on the monuments, etc., she just packaged the whole thing and took it to some fifteen different sponsors. Seeing the digital interest that has already been aroused, one of them took the hook...that's it.'

Malati, leaning further back in her chair with her ankles crossed and her fingers steepled, is the very picture of breezy confidence. There is, however, almost two decades between 'this girl' and me. Twenty years in which the world has been taken over by Google, Facebook, YouTube, blogs and what not. Twenty years in which I have progressed from laborious longhand to a two-finger 'search and peck' on a keyboard to reading and answering emails and of course to scouring Google. Yes, I can see what this girl has done but no, I cannot do it.

'Ah! I see. Not up to the task, are you, Mr B? So, that's it, isn't it? Well, don't worry, I understand perfectly. I can do it for you, you know. I mean my distant nephew can. He is a developer and a social marketeer, we could set up a "Grievances about Glenmont Greens" site and can have it SEO'ed and everything else. Meaning that every time Glenmont Greens is googled, this will come right on top and we could make an interactive site around it. This will become the virtual meeting point of everyone who's been shafted by this developer and a forum for creating change. Abhishek, my nephew, also has a lot of other tools and tricks to ensure that this is always talked about. Then, all of you guys can have an offline meeting to decide what to do. Why should you take it lying down?'

Short, jerky steps are pacing this narration. As the business case is being built up, so is the excitement. Malati has left the chair she was sitting on and has been pacing up and down in front of me as she is working out her strategy on how best to build up a credible opposition to the developer's one-sided stranglehold on the situation. While she is doing this—entirely of her own volition and completely to help our cause—I am eyeing the lively undulations in the silk blouse she is wearing. How as she walks towards me, the cups of her bra get outlined on each step forward and how the blouse gets filled in each time a foot comes down.

Is it true, I wonder, that as women get older, their breasts swing more from side to side rather than bob up and down? Or is it merely a function of fullness? Or perhaps of the walk? As she walks away, the view, if anything, is even better. The question here is only one—if she is not wearing a thong, how can I not see a panty line? The material of the pants is certainly thin enough.

Do I really deserve a home? Here is this lady who, albeit worked up by her own excitement, is actually doing me nothing but a favour and here I am thinking more and more like a male stray dog. The type that survives on scraps and runs hopefully behind every raised tail. Don't I just deserve to curl up on any available space on the pavement? Why the Gurgaon condo? Malati has been at pains to take me through Mr Biswas's journey and his noble pursuit of putting down a credible anchor. All I have are lascivious thoughts without even the resolve of carrying them to culmination. Stray dogs remain nameless—maybe she has divined the connection—and that's why I'll forever remain the nameless Mr B to her.

♠

Day 253

IT IS ALREADY the second week of October, but there is no sign of autumnal pleasantness, either in the weather or in my life. A stifling heat still has Delhi in its vice-like grip. There is an enervating grey-brown layer of dust and precipitated pollution on everything. It's as if the skies themselves rain this fine grey soot that seeps into every space and covers every surface. After touching anything, including the handle of the car door while opening it, the fingers itch to be wiped on a clean piece of cloth. Even the leaves of every tree and every bush are covered with this greyness. However, the seemingly meaningless rush of the city continues. Every morning, people get into their cars or perch themselves atop their two-wheelers and rush, honking and abusing, into the roaring rivers of traffic. Risking life and limb, sacrificing every last ounce of mental peace, breathing in the greyness, they arrive at their offices after having triumphed over the combat in the streets. There, they join another fight—the fight that is the average man's average working day—a fight that is fought daily in the hundreds of thousands of offices and workplaces that after having strangulated Delhi have now cancerously galloped all over the National Capital Region. Little wonder then that everybody is always at an edge here—tetchy, irritable, unable to consider another's point of view, quick to take offence and always ready to attack first and ask questions later.

'I think that is a really bad idea. It'll never work.'

'Who the hell are you to criticize my ideas anyway? It's not as if you've shown any brilliance with yours.'

'Please just stop talking, the two of you, and listen to me.'

'Can we please have some order here? We have a common problem. Can we at least try to arrive at a common solution?'

'Listen. Listen, just listen—we have circulated an agenda earlier. Can't we just stick to it instead of fighting amongst ourselves?'

'We will never get anywhere. We are just helping the developer, not ourselves.'

The bedlam and the chaos of the city have caught up with us, our newly minted community. Malati's nephew—a twenty-year-old, long-haired hippy-kind of person—has worked wonders with his laptop. We now have a group and our 'Grievances against Glenmont Greens' or gagg.com is a wildly successful Internet community. Within days of its creation, it has hundreds of posts and although the bulk of them are from real estate dealers offering never heard before deals on never heard before properties in Gurgaon, many of them are from genuine buyers of the dreams that Glenmont Greens promised. And all of them are aggrieved—vociferously, argumentatively and combatively aggrieved. This is the first 'offline' meeting of the group. It is happening in the community centre of an apartment complex in Gurgaon; one of the buyers is a tenant in this complex and has offered the community centre as a meeting venue. Roshni and I too—me being digitally invisible as one of the creators of the group—are here as duped home-owners. Sadly, this meeting, much like Glenmont Greens, seems to be headed nowhere. Although, most of the attendees are fairly young and successful corporate types, all that has been happening so far is bitter argument. Globally-renowned Indian management talent is displaying its inability to work as a team.

'I am a retired Wing Commander of the Indian Air Force. My name is Harjinder Singh. I am 65 years old. I request your attention. Those in favour of legal action, please raise your right hands.'

Tall, ramrod straight, with a snow-white beard and moustache, and wearing a white shirt, dark purple tie, blue turban and a blue suit, this elderly Sikh gentleman has a dignity all of his own. The traditional Indian deference to seniority coupled with the power of the gentleman's personality force the many raised voices in the room into an uneasy silence.

'My wife and I need a place to stay in. If we can come to an agreement, then we will be a force that the developer will have to consider. The sooner we do this, the sooner we can have our flats. The sooner my wife and I will have our home. For us, it is very urgent to have this home now. I have more than 30 years of administrative experience and I am offering my services to coordinate our efforts.'

A smattering of applause and 'hear, hears' follow the Wing Commander's address. Within the next half hour, a consensus on the way forward is worked out. Legal action is ruled out as of now. In the wisdom of the group, an appeal to the law is premature and should be used only as the last resort. It is agreed that within the next week, a delegation of owners led by our redoubtable Wg Cdr (Retd) Harjinder Singh will meet the developer, present our case and petition for a resumption of the building's construction. As we are leaving, I notice to my consternation and swiftly rising panic that Malati is in the room.

Demurely clad in an earth-coloured salwar kameez, with the chunni covering her hair and face and wearing large shades over her eyes, Malati has been there from the beginning of the meeting. Dressed as she was, I had completely missed her earlier in the crowd of absolutely unfamiliar faces. When she notices that I have, at last, seen her and that Roshni is busy collecting and distributing visiting cards, she gives me an enigmatic smile, bunches her fist, puts it next to her ear and sticks out the thumb and the little finger in the universally recognized symbol of 'we'll talk on the phone'. She exits the community centre before us.

'So, what do you think will happen now? With this officer gentleman leading our charge, do you think that construction will restart?'

'God knows there are enough half-done buildings in this city already, ours could well become just another one. Remember what FatBum said, *"bhoot bangla".'*

'The money is stuck right? If we choose to get out now, what will happen? Nothing, right? Will the fellow return our money? No? And nobody will ever buy it from us. Why should they? When so much of new construction is happening all around and so many new flats are available, who'd want to buy it from another person when they can buy straight from the builders themselves? And the EMIs will keep going from the bank, no matter what, right?'

Asking and answering her own questions, Roshni seems to be plunging deeper and deeper into a black mood. I have no new answers as these are the very questions that I have been battling with for months now. Our money is stuck. We are stuck. Worse, if we do get unstuck and the project takes off, then we are stuck forever in this place. Stuck in this interminable traffic, breathing these toxic fumes, slowly being driven to the edge of madness by the constant honking and complete lawlessness on the roads, bouncing from one pothole to the other to arrive at a gated apartment complex where captive generators supply the electricity, captive gas banks supply cooking gas and a sewage treatment plant treats our waste. It sounds surreal, but that's what it will be, an island separate and apart from the city. That's what most residential projects here are. They have no connection to any municipal services, no connection to any of the amenities that one would normally take for granted in any city. They have no connection simply because these services do not exist here. Fittingly, Kenny Rogers and Dolly Parton are singing 'Islands in the Stream' through the cars music system and Roshni is turning the music up to drown out the silence between us.

'Be careful. Our turn is coming up on the left soon and these trucks are not going to move. You better turn on your left indicator light and move behind that truck now.'

As if battling the trucks and the traffic were not enough, here I have a side-seat driver too. It's not as if I do not know that the turn is coming up or that I lack the experience of these roads to know that I need to make my move now. Suppressing my irritation at these superfluous instructions, I choose not to react to Roshni's statements because after all, what she is saying is right and I do have to sneak in between two trucks to make it to my turn on time.

'By the way, who was that lady smiling at you and gesturing that you should call her?'

The car nearly crashes into the truck. Swerving at the last minute, I try consciously to take deep breaths, slow my heart down and gather my thoughts. Obviously, Roshni has seen. Obviously, she knows. No, that is not obvious because there is nothing to know. And why should I lie again? Or be defensive?

'Oh that! That was just Malati, you know, Malati Patel? The Eng Lit teacher?'

'No. Actually, I don't. You see, we have never been introduced. And what was "just" Malati doing there? How is it that she was "just there"? Or perhaps, she too has bought a flat there. That would be so cosy, *na*? Perhaps you could "just" commute to work together?'

'Roshni, now, you are just overreacting. I think Malati was there with her nephew. After all, they have a reason to be there. They need to check too.'

'Nephew? Reason? Check what?'

Too late, I realize I have said too much now and too little earlier. Roshni's tone is sharp, monosyllabic and interrogative. It leaves me with no room to backtrack. My best option is to come clean. Full disclosure is the need of the hour and I do not hold back. I give Roshni every last detail of what I know which in any case is not too much as I do not know how the process works. The only thing that I am sure of is that it is to our benefit and it is obviously successful.

'You mean you shared all this—our personal problems—with your colleague? And found solutions too?'

'No. I mean yes. It was a general conversation on how these builders are rooking us and then her nephew offered to help. It's just a sort of experiment he's doing.'

'You did not think it necessary to tell me? To involve me in all of this? I mean, am I supposed to be a part of this house or not? What do you think you are doing? And who exactly is she to "help" us out? What is happening here? What the hell are you up to?'

'But, but, I didn't do anything. That boy did everything. I did not even agree or disagree. He just asked me some questions and put up the website himself. After that, it's all happening by itself. And, it's happening for the good, don't you see?'

'Aahaha! You did not do anything, that boy did everything. What are you? Some nursery school student in short pants? Look teacher, that boy did everything. I did not do anything. I only spent hours chatting up my hot colleague and giving her intimate details of my domestic issues only to get her sympathies, only to make her feel warm towards me. No matter that I have a wife at home. How does that change anything? I did not do anything? It's all happening for the good. Yes, I see what is happening. I see everything.'

Roshni has wound herself up. Now there will be no stopping her till we get home. It is useless even trying to get a word in edgeways. The river is in full spate and in this condition it is better to just let it flow. Whatever I say, can and will be held against me. Each of my words will be cruelly twisted, mimicked and thrown back at me. Silence is the best policy, and in any case, the road requires my full attention. However, I cannot help but feel wronged. Some kid's experiment in social media, which I thought would be too insignificant to report to my wife, is costing us too much. But isn't it helping us at the same time? Gagg.com is what is lifting the veils off nefarious builders and creating an entire community. So what if it's shutting me off from my wife? I guess that's the nature of the beast. That which heals also hurts. Every sword is double-edged.

'You can take your beer-drinking best friend and solve all your problems with her. I am going out for a week now. Have fun. Have a lot of fun.'

We have reached home and Roshni has just banged the bedroom door shut in my face. Of course, she is going out for a week; she has fashion shows lined up in three cities and has been working on this project for months now. Of course, I know of this and have been wishing and praying for her success too. Only, I did not visualize the send-off to her trip to be anything like this. Suddenly, interrupting my thoughts, a cell phone chimes. It's a WhatsApp message on Roshni's cell phone, the same phone that she, in her anger, has left along with her bag on the dining room table while she stomped off to the bedroom.

To give the phone to her, I pick it up and notice that the WhatsApp message is still on the screen. It is an image...of Rocky. Bare-bodied, flexing his muscles, wearing just a pair of shorts and posing. As I hold the phone in dumbfounded amazement, more images pour in. Rocky in all sorts of poses... some in close-ups, some with dressy clothes, some in swimwear, some with menacing looks, some, the Greek God type. The last is accompanied with a caption—'Here you go. Hope these work for you. The Rock'. Gradually, the images dim and the phone screen goes dark again. I carefully replace the phone on the table and slowly walk out of the house and down the stairs. Goodbye, Roshni. All the best for your week-long trip.

Day 274

$\mathcal{A}$T LONG LAST the temperatures are cooling down. The five days of Durga Puja have descended with all the fervour that transplanted colonies of Bengalis can summon and every year, it seems to get more ostentatiously festive and less traditionally Bengali. As usual, we have been reached out to for contributions, for participation and for managing as has always been ever since we have lived here. For the first time, Roshni has declined any sort of participation. She has been travelling, been busy, does not have the time, does not have the energy, is not in the mood... 'Here is my financial contribution, the *chanda*,' and that's all she has to give. She is now sharing office space with a friend who has a studio in Hauz Khas Village and more and more she prefers to spend time there. Unlike her, my fears, my suspicions, indeed my certainties, no longer rise to the surface to get refreshed by the cold air of articulation. They remain buried. They fester. They feed upon themselves and in a monstrously cancerous reproductive process, breed shadowy replicas. I know that the images that now dance their perverted tango inside my consciousness bear little resemblance to the originals.

Maddeningly however, no matter how valiant my attempts, I am powerless to stop my diseased imaginings. Slowly, they secrete their corrosive poison and it seeps through everything, infecting, corrupting, polluting, and sometimes paralyzing every thought and every action.

'You know, I took you for granted, son. You have always been the best singer in our group. And nobody really gets Hemanta's songs like you do. I was so looking forward to settling down in the back row and keeping time with my hip flask to your version of "Runner". Now, for the local talent section they'll have some Probashi fool who'll sing Bengali songs with a Hindi accent.'

I have nothing to say to Mr Mukherjee. I have no emotions for him either except for a sort of pity. A pity that has guilt woven deeply into it; guilt that I should be responsible for stealing away the one bright spot that he so looks forward to and pity that this bright spot should be my singing. Mr Mukherjee—sorry, still defiantly Mr Mukhopadhyay—a widower of ten years now, lives with his son, who is now 'Mukherji', and his 'Hindustani' wife Sapna. Mrs S Mukherji nee Prasad is clear and stridently vocal about the fact that her father-in-law's presence in the house is an unwanted intrusion in her life and his habits and manners a pernicious influence on her darling boy, a snot-nosed, spoilt-rotten ten-year-old brat. After almost three decades in the army, retiring as a subedar major, Mr Mukhopadhyay's speech is liberally peppered with the only Hindi he knows, which is little more than a collection of imaginatively abusive epithets, and his evenings liberally sprinkled with army ration issue XXX Hercules Rum. Retreating in the face of feminine firepower, this aged soldier now pours libation on his lonely soul in the great outdoors. It is a sad sight to see the old man sitting on a bench in the evenings, swigging silently from a hip flask as the Delhi dust swirls around him. A sapper decorated for valour in Jaffna as part of the Indian infantry expeditionary force, he now keeps vigil over the dogs which are brought to this treeless, grassless park everyday by the dog walkers of the rich in the colony for their evening shit. I know him well because I sometimes give company to his drinking with my smoking. But no, I cannot sing for him this Durga Puja. In fact, I cannot remember when I sang last. I do not know when I will sing next.

'Is all okay with you? Come, come, give an old man some company. I can see that you are alone too and looking really lost. Let's walk around the pandal together.'

'See, that is where the ladies used to set up the food stalls. I used to love the *kosha mangsho* and *loochi* here. Aha! Just thinking about those days makes my mouth water. Of course, now it's all Kake Da this and Bappe Da that. Do you know how much of a profit is made by the committee simply letting out these food stalls during the Puja. Preposterous! Isn't it? And, *cholo, cholo, Pronam koro* young man. There's Ma Durga's *protima*. Thankfully, they still have Ma Durga's *protima*. In some pandals, I am told even this has changed and has become hindified. However, I am blessed, I have a Ma Durga at home, you know, the very personification of Shakti. Of course, there I am, the Mahishasura. *Pronam hoyeche*? All blessings taken? Let us now check the programme. You are refusing to sing tonight, so let's see whose screeching I will be subjected to. Let's also go get some mutton chops.'

This warrior seems to have come loaded to the battle. As I get closer, my nose confirms for me that, yes indeed, this engine is already tanked up. XXX Hercules is sending scent signals to anyone within a two-foot radius.

'Here we are with the mutton chops. Now what we need are two bottles of Coca-Cola. Here, you hang on to these... careful, they're hot. I'll get the Coke.'

Remarkably sprightly for his age, the old man comes back in five minutes triumphantly holding up two plastic bottles of Coca-Cola like he's holding up the regimental colours. I know exactly what he is doing. He is going to pour some of the Coca-

Cola into the ground, make up the difference in each bottle from the contents of his flask, expect me to 'liberate' two chairs from the tent and bring them to his spot under the only tree in the area and join him in savouring the Rum Coke, the mutton chops and the delights of his conversation. I know this because he has invited me many times earlier to join him and every time I have declined. Today, however, I am tempted. If I am to soldier on with life being the way it is, why not trade notes with an older soldier? At least, this is not Tubluda, this is not going to become an 'extended education class' where I will be made to feel my own ignorance at every point. Plus, Roshni is not coming home tonight too. There is one more fitting session and night-long rehearsals for yet another fashion show at a studio in West Delhi, at least that's what her WhatsApp says.

'My sergeant used to say, there's a difference between shitting and shitting your pants. My CO, a superb officer, an officer's son himself, was very polished. Before we went on our final push in Jaffna, he explained to us that there is a difference between fear and being scared. Fear is human, not in your control. Being scared, however, is in your control. Similarly, my boy, there is sadness. And then, there is being sad. Sadness is the human condition. Being sad is in your control. You, my friend, are being sad. Get over your sadness. Of course you can conquer it. Out of control? Everything is always out of control. Who are you to control things anyway? Just try to keep yourself in control. Isn't that more than enough for any human being?'

We've been drinking and chatting for a while now. The lights in the tent have dimmed. The food stalls are empty. Stray dogs are nosing for scraps in the rubbish that has accumulated ankle-deep behind the stands. The last of the overdressed, overweight people are leaving. Now the cleaning crew will come in and they will all be as underfed as underdressed. The strains of the singers of the 'Local Talent Show' had wafted across the night air to where we were sitting. We were glad to be sitting so far away, they were truly atrocious. Now, the projector and the screen are being set up for the night's movie. It will have a thin attendance. There are far too many and far more comfortable entertainment choices nowadays. The lights have a red glow around them. The heavier, colder air is trapping the dust, particulate matter and automobile exhaust and bringing it down to ground level. Around the lights, it has a weirdly polarizing effect creating alternating swirling halos of redness and blueness. The second hip flask has made an appearance and the subterfuge of Coca-Cola has been abandoned. The old soldier has breached my defences and in successive sorties has learnt of my lonely jousts against Glenmont Greens, of my rallying forces through gagg. com, of the Wing Commander's unsuccessful sally against the developer—yes, basically the developer has challenged us to do our worst, he will do what he can, when he can. Till then, we can huff and puff and threaten to blow his house down but he is not going to move. More than that, we have traded notes on our personal lives too and my domestic unhappiness floats on the surface of the conversation like the bubbles in the Rum Coke we are drinking. It rises from the bottom, appears on the surface, pops and disappears into the thin air. His situation at home, while poignantly sad to us who view it from the outside, does not seem to worry him in the slightest. On the contrary, he seems to be vastly amused at my concern.

'I have a place to shelter from the elements, a warm bed, and hot food. What'll I do with prestige, self-respect and the other bullshit you keep spouting? Can I eat it? Can I wear it? Why should I be disappointed? Sapna *Bouma* (daughter-in-law) is what she is. Please understand, she is the one who is distressed with the situation, not me. Anyway, so much of tension and stress you have that you can't even enjoy a drink! With all this headache, why do you even want to build a house? You were talking of peace and happiness? Four concrete walls and a roof will give you that?'

'Well, I don't want to sit on a bench drinking rum all by myself.'

'You could be in a palace and still you would be by yourself… and perhaps not with peace and happiness for company. You think a house will bring you happiness? At least, clarify your goals. Your goal is the house. That's fine. That's a goal. Don't then claim that your goal is happiness. You don't know what will bring that. We were luckier. We knew our goals. Clear that hill. Make sure that every last militant is dead—dee ee aaye dee—in this village. Simple. What was the overall objective? Was it senseless murder? That was the officer's job to figure out. Is this going to win the war? Is it going to create everlasting peace? That's the general's job. Actually, it's the politician's wish…or maybe not. You are trying to be the politician and the general together. Get happiness. Create peace. These are big ones. You are trying to be both and shooting for the big ones while actually doing the soldier's job, that is, building a house. What do you think? That'll get you peace and happiness? Be clear. You want more Coke? Clear the village. Gain the hill. Build the house. These are clear. Will it win the war? Create peace and happiness in your life? Bring you joy forever? Leave that to the generals, sonny boy, or the politicians. Actually, they are the same after a point. Another mutton chop? Sorry, the stall is closed.'

The projector has been switched off. The screen folded up. The only audience was the local labour lads and the one lonely member of the organizing committee who was certainly not going to waste his sleep over showing them a film in a language they would not in any case understand. We are alone now. The world seems to have gone to sleep. After the day's hectic activity in this area, the silence seems louder. The only lights are from the gate arch announcing the chief sponsors name and the lighting around the idols. Mr Mukhopadhyay's face is luridly lit by alternating strobes of red and green light as he leans forward to speak and is illuminated by the pulsating colours of the sponsor's logo.

'Happiness, sonny, is your rifle, your water bottle and your ammunition belt. You better make sure that these are with you when you are dodging the bullets of life. Because when you get shot, and get shot you will if you live long enough, all you want is a drink of water...and hell, you would want to shoot back. The good thing is that you can carry these with you. Happiness is portable. It is yours to carry. Most of us make the mistake of thinking it's a destination or what you call a goal or objective. It's not. It's something you carry with you...or not. The best thing is that sooner or later you get to a Forward Base. And there, you can always refill your bottle and rearm your rifle. And then, you are good to go again. My Forward Base tonight was your singing Hemanta's "Runner". That didn't happen. But guess what? I found another Base—this session we're having. So, now I'm ready for another week at the front line.'

I do not trust myself to speak. I do not have the old veteran's seemingly limitless capacity and know that now my slurring tongue cannot keep pace with my soaring thoughts. In any case, Mr Mukhopadhyay only seems to need an occasional nod and grunt to carry on afresh. Once again, I think how wrong we are with our assumptions and presumptions. Here is the man who we all took for granted as being lonely and unhappy giving me lessons on happiness. He has never been lonely. He has always had himself for company. While here I am, seeking company with Roshni and Malati and looking for happiness in a house...

or finding unhappiness in a WhatsApp image.

'But go ahead and build that house. That you must do. If you have set yourself an objective, you must achieve it. That house needs to be built.'

I don't believe I am hearing the old man right. Is it the alcohol again?

'But all this time you have been saying that I will not find happiness, not find peace in building a house. I thought you meant that building the house is an exercise in waste.'

'Rubbish. Have you understood nothing? Take the wool out of your ears. Listen carefully. What I have been trying to explain to you is that happiness is not connected to this. It is linked to nothing. Happiness is what you carry with you. That does not mean you do not build the house. What's the confusion? You live in the world, you must do what the world does. The world builds houses. So, you must build a house too. Just don't link happiness with it the way the world does. That's all I have been saying.'

Once again, this is a Tubluda moment. Once again, I am feeling like an idiot child. But then again, it is not a Tubluda moment. There is something more than an algebra equation being clarified here. There is a deeper comprehension of life's realities that the old man is articulating here. Or perhaps the Hercules is making everything weightier than it actually is.

'Ah, but you didn't. You live in your son's house.' Before I realize what I am saying, I've blurted this out. This is definitely below the belt and gratuitously hurtful to the old man. However, he does not even blink. Ever the soldier, he just absorbs the blow, leans forward and smiles.

'What make you so sure? What makes you think I didn't? How else do you think that Sapna Bouma's house got built?'

Day 295

ʟADIES AND GENTLEMEN, imagine yourselves transported 700 years back in history. Geographically, the place is exactly the same. You have just left behind the fort of Ghiyasuddin Tughlaq where you have watched the heads of criminals being crushed under the feet of elephants in the royal court at Tughluqabad. You have exchanged gifts with Ibn Batuta and hope that you will be everlastingly enshrined in his memoirs because you know that he is a famed traveller and writer. The tower of victory—Qutab Minar—made a scant century ago is clearly visible in front of you over the scrub and thorn forests. Maybe you can even discern the tomb of Balban right here in Mehrauli. You are now searching for the road to the north because you need to dip yourself or perhaps slake your thirst in the royal tank—the Hauz Khas—but you are fearful, worried about your well-being, indeed, your life. It is already mid-morning. You definitely need to spur your horses and reach before evening because the forests in between are dangerous. Some say they are even haunted by the ghosts of the ten thousand Mongols beheaded by Alauddin Khilji, less than fifty years ago, to built his city of skulls—to lay waste peaceful Mongol Puri and create the fort of heads—Siri Fort.

'Seven centuries later and your progress is just as slow and just as dangerous, not because of the forests, the wild animals and the wilder marauding bands of Gujars and Jats—well, those too—but more because you, my friends and fellow twenty-first-century students, are now stuck in some of the world's worst traffic and are breathing what is without doubt the world's most dangerous air.'

'He's very good, isn't he?' Malati, sitting on my left, looks up at me and asks. Disconcertingly, her breath smells of fresh mint, 'Oh yes, indeed. He makes the history of this city come alive. Certainly does a much better job of it than I could have'. I have to consciously look a little away when I speak because I know that my breath smells of stale tobacco smoke.

We are all crammed into a bus travelling through the city. This is yet another of the college's Art Council's initiatives—The Humanities Tour of Delhi. The idea is to not waste the winter and to use the weather to familiarize the students with the living history that we are all so fortunate to be a part of. Different students take on the role of guides on different days and today we have truly found a genius. Part showman, part scholar, full-time show-off, Ankit Garg is a find for our department. He is helming this tour and doing a superb job of it. This is supposed to finish off at the Lodi Gardens, where the other humanities subject—literature—will kick in. Poetry will be read and a Shakespearean scene will be performed. The class will move out of the classroom. The study of humanities will be humanized. The students will learn because they will live the lesson and not just read it.

All this sounded so good when we talked of it in the staffroom. So good, in fact, that the principal signed off on it without any questions and not just that, he even suggested that it should be included as a part of the 'Best Practices' to be presented to the Governing Body of the Academic Council and be institutionalized as an annual feature for all colleges in the university. Even the students were enthusiastic enough to sign on en masse for the tour and to find a bus sponsor for it on their own initiative. However, the reality is very different from the rosy picture everyone painted.

Delhi seems to have finally given up. Like he has with everything else, modern man has triumphed here too. First, we, as a species, wiped out more species than anything else since the dawn of life on the planet. Of course, we did not spare ourselves either and learning avidly from the World Wars refined the practice of industrial human slaughter to a point of terrifying efficiency. Next, we trained our sights on the environment and the world at large. By dumping millions of tons of waste into the land and the oceans, and pumping millions of tons of gases into the air, we poisoned all three. Now, we have sharpened the focus of those sights on to the cities we live in. And Delhi has been hit the hardest. Bravely battling on since the time of being called Indraprastha, and then recovering from the purges of the Islamic sword as well as the Christian cannon, this seat of power—my beloved old lady who I was so hopeful of up to the beginning of the year—seems to have finally thrown in the towel. She seems to have accepted defeat and is now lying belly-up in supine acceptance, awaiting the inevitable coup de grâce. In the meantime, the traffic writhes and throbs on her surface like a billion maggots draining away her life blood; the skies—pregnant with their load of pollution lower down on her, cutting off any life-giving air and suffocating her with an aerial blanket of poison; and the water—black, viscous and noisome leaches out of her from thousands of suppurating cuts to frothily corrupt the river that sustained her for millennia.

We created the city. Now, we are killing it.

Today we are one of those maggots of traffic stuck on the road breathing in the malodorous exhausts of the others and occasionally writhing and jerking in some pathetic imitation of forward movement. Even Ankit's genius cannot hold our attention forever but such is the magic of youth that middle-aged depressions like mine do not find an easy purchase on their minds. The minute Ankit finishes, a song competition starts, the traditional Indian *antakshari*. Now, whether the traffic moves or not, whether Lodi Gardens is reached or not, whether the poems are recited or the plays enacted, there will be happiness here. Maybe that old subedar major was right. Maybe we do carry it with ourselves.

Last week, Malati was not on the bus. Neither was Ankit and his garrulous genius. After languishing in traffic for more than an hour, I had deserted my post and got off the bus at South Extension. From there, I walked to Defence Colony and tried to visualize for myself Subedar Major Pabitra Mukhopadhyays predicament at his retirement from the army, a tale that was still ringing in my ears ten days after it was told to me through the course of one Herculean night.

Two Mukhopadhyay brothers had joined the army, the oldest and the youngest. Separated by a gap of twenty-five years, the younger was no doubt in awe of the elder who would visit the family home in the village once a year and spend two months drinking rum and telling tales of derring-do in lands far away. Certainly, the little one was awestruck enough to follow his brother's footsteps, wear the same uniform, and more than fifty years later, tell a drunken tale of happiness and home ownership to a somewhat angry and confused middle-aged man on a Mahashtami night that is, me. The material difference between the two was that while the older brother remained a lifelong bachelor, the younger one got married and raised a family.

Havildar Pijush Mukhopadhyay, the older brother, was a

soldier who fought in the '65 war against Pakistan. Even while bullets were being exchanged on the Western Front, the city of Delhi was being relentlessly built and growing exponentially to accommodate the millions that Lutyens never envisioned. South of Lodi Colony, where government servants were accommodated, was the housing colony earmarked to be settled by the intrepid veterans of the armed forces. Imaginatively named 'Defence Colony', it was presumed that the courageous members of the military would willingly stake their claims on this wilderness and build homes for their families where jackals roamed. While the big plots of C and D blocks were 'senior officer' territory, the small and smaller plots of A block were open to NCOs and JCOs. Havildar Mukhopadhyay learnt of all this while crouched with his officer in a slit trench on the front line with shells flying overhead. The officer had made the down payment for a 325-square-yard corner plot in C Block and in the unguarded camaraderie of a hole in the ground with death in the air and hot sweet tea for company, urged his sergeant to similarly build a permanent place for the still-living of his family to ensure a foothold in the National Capital. That is how A 261, Defence Colony came into Mukhopadhyay possession.

Last week, after getting off the bus, I had walked up to the address to see for myself if any of that poignant history remained. The short answer is no, of course not. The small plot now has a three-storey structure on it with a basement. The basement is a beauty parlour, the first floor, a computer coaching centre and the top two floors are residences. The single-level two rooms around a central drawing room, the backyard with the handpump, the guava tree and the grapevines, the verandah on the front where the havildar had placed his hookah—all that has of course disappeared. Even more troublesome to me was that I could not even imagine it ever having been there.

In the din of Delhi traffic, amidst the shoving and jostling of the pedestrians on the sidewalk, sneezing continuously in the ground-level fog of airborne dust and auto exhaust smoke, I just could not visualize the picture that the subedar major had painted of the *grihaprabesh* of the two brothers' home in Defence Colony. Neither could I visualize an arrangement where one brother pays for the plot with his army retirement benefits, while simultaneously another starts paying for the construction of the house with his salary on starting military service. And now, the house belongs to them jointly and in equal measure. I guess it was all simpler, even doable, because the havildar never got married and never raised a family. Conveniently perhaps, in five years he passed away and Mr Mukhopadhyay became the sole owner of a home in Defence Colony, South Delhi. Yes, he had built his own home in Delhi. No, he never stayed there to enjoy it, there were no home postings. Yes, his son—the Mr Mukherji, husband of Sapna Mukherji nee Prasad—did grow up there. No, as an adult he never saw it as home, at least, his wife did not. Yes, Mr Mukhopadhyay's wife died there. No, he could never have stayed there forever, even after his retirement.

'Don't you see? The joys of living in your own home can never match the joys that your relatives would get if the money made from selling that home could be theirs to share. The problem was that the Defence Colony property rates became too high. When the value rises so much, then the home is not seen as a just a home, it becomes an encashable investment. I was told that I was wasting the investment by sitting on it. Apparently, living in my own home was a waste!!'

That day, as I walked around the block and turned into the market to treat myself to a chocolate pastry from Defence Bakery, the old man's words kept coming back to me. Yes, indeed, the house had become too big an asset for him to reconcile with his simple ways and too juicily attractive to be left idle by his grown-up son and daughter-in-law. So, it had to go. It was fated to go. Its time was up. Its job was done. On Mrs Mukhopadhyay's dying wishes, it was sold to pay for the South Delhi 'builder flat' for her darling son and of course Mr Mukhopadhyay would always have a place to stay with his son, wouldn't he? The rest of the money could always be locked away in a deposit for the grandchildren. So, in one fell swoop, Mr Mukhopadhyay lost his home while Mr Mukherji gained one. The balance, as always, was maintained. Happiness, like his water bottle and spare ammunition, the old man carried with himself. That was never part of the equation.

'Gagg.com seems to be working, you know. The builder has too much online public pressure on him now. His other projects are suffering. He's made a statement in a press release yesterday.'

While I have been ruminating on last week, the bus has at last reached its destination. We have reached Lodi Gardens and there is a picnic atmosphere as groups of laughing, singing students are getting off the bus shepherded by the indefatigable Ankit. Malati, now sensitive to my moods, has held off talking while I have been lost in my thoughts. Only now, as the bus has stopped and we are all getting off, has she spoken.

"Really! That's wonderful. Somehow, I seem to have missed it. What's he said? Is he restarting the building?'

'Apparently he has got some foreign funding for his company now. He has tied up with some Singapore-based developer to bring FDI into the "Smart Cities Programme". Also, as an aside, he has stated that some of the temporary issues that had crept into one of his company's Gurgaon developments have now been ironed out and work has resumed in full swing. Presumably, he is referring to Glenmont Greens.'

Lodi Gardens is 90 acres of peace and tranquility in the

midst of the city's turbulent chaos. It is an oasis of calm that the Imperial British administration had created by the simple expedient of 'relocating' the villages that had sprung up around the ruins of the tombs erected between five and six hundred years ago. As we admire Lady Willingdon's landscaping, breathe in the fresh air and walk down the rolling greens to the resplendently restored tombs, my mood lifts. It is also because of the news Malati has just brought in. I share with her my thought of how easy it would be to be a builder if one were a Mughal Emperor or a British Governor General. Then, we would not be messing around with small fry like Glenmont Greens and worrying ourselves sick over public opinion, consumer pressure, Internet groups, urban infrastructure and sundry other minor irritants. Oh no, then it would be the Taj Mahals or entire cities for us. Protests? Behead the buggers if we were the Mughals, create an Instrument of Accession or a Document of Appropriation if we were the British, of course, signing it as Your Most Humble Obedient Servant. Life must have been easier in those times. Malati is quick to remind me that rather than being the Emperor or the Governor General, chances are that I would have been amongst the 'beheaded' or the 'accessed' and the 'appropriated'. Perhaps life would not then be so easy? Perhaps life has never been easy.

Day 316

OUR ELEVENTH WEDDING anniversary has come and gone. It has passed by without even a murmur in our lives. I remember clearly that bitterly cold day in the first week of December, eleven years ago, when a bearded bookish Bengali heading into his thirties defied the conventions he had been brought up in to marry a dewily pretty young fashion designer from Meerut who had come to Delhi for her undergraduate studies and had stayed back for a professional designing course but ended up making, what everyone in her family maintained, a disastrously wrong matrimonial choice. No one from either of our families was present. Lots of friends, lots of good wishes and lots of alcohol was the marriage send-off that Roshni and I received. Being absolutely indigent—I was not yet 'permanent' as a lecturer and the bride was just starting out in the fashion design profession—we had asked all our friends to give us 'cash only, no presents please'. Our wedding night was spent in the bedroom of our two-room rooftop *barsati* huddled under two blankets and a single quilt emptying out the envelopes we had received and counting out the cash while the two-bar electric heater and our love bathed the peeling walls, the cracked concrete floor and the iron-grilled windows in a warm glow. We had received 44,312 rupees. We were infinitely rich. We were infinitely happy.

'The bank has raised the interest rate. Something to do with the RBI Lending Rate or what is this? Something called BPLR or Benchmark Prime Lending Rate. We had chosen to go with the floating rate, not fixed, and now either we increase the amount of the EMIs we're paying or we pay for a longer tenure.'

Roshni was sitting in the sunlit spot on the drawing room sofa. The morning beams were lighting her from behind. Dressed in a housecoat with a sweater on top, eyes still puffy with sleep, hair pulled up in a tight bun on her head with a pin through it, fluffy woolen socks on her feet which were folded up and tucked beneath her, she had all the previous weeks' bills and letters strewn around her on the sofa. The few hair that had escaped from the tight bun were dancing about her neck and shoulders, glinting silver in the sunbeams. I remember how conscious she has become of these few grey hairs now—the first signs of ageing—and all appearing in the course of the past six months.

'Happy Anniversary, Roshni,' I had said as I put the teacup on the table and went to join her on the sofa.

'We've exchanged greetings in the morning already. Let's move on. We have bigger things to think about now. What are we going to do with this? A larger EMI or a longer tenure? Or are we going to need to seek advice on this too? I don't think you are concentrating enough on this. Maybe if you spoke to the bank this interest rate change could be avoided? Or perhaps another bank could give us a better rate?'

That was our eleventh wedding anniversary, an occasion that had succumbed to the fatal attraction of an interest rate change.

Why are all of us not able to pack only our happy memories into our water bottles and ammunition pouches? Because then I would only remember sprinting up three floors to a rooftop, shouldering open a *barsati* door and up-ending a jute sack on the floor. It was the jute sack that I had been carrying on my back while running up the stairs, the same jute sack that was packed to bursting with the twelve gift-wrapped packages it contained, one to celebrate each month of our marriage. I would remember an ecstatically happy Roshni flinging herself on to me, wrapping both her legs around my hips and smothering my face with kisses. I would remember our conversations. I would remember our silences. I would remember our candlelit 'treat' dinners. I would remember our Maggi noodles lunches. I would remember our motorcycle rides. I would remember our drunken giggles on the backseats of taxis. I would not remember accidentally intercepted WhatsApp images.

Roshni, on a matter of principle, does not want to pay the bank one *naya paisa* more than what we had signed on for. The fact that we had chosen a floating-rate loan option was immaterial for her. I had once again contacted my 'top-up home loan' agent friend, Abhijeet Prasad, and requested him to come to our rescue. Roshni had, in turn, poured her heart out to FatBum and he had fielded his sister's nephew's brother-in-law—the one who 'works in the Janakpuri branch'—bank clerk. The face-off happened three days ago in our flat with Roshni, FatBum and myself in attendance. At stake was the way forward for us with our home loan and where to fix that damned floating point of interest rate. The gladiators were ranged around the dining table and Roshni and I, to mix metaphors, were like the seconds of jousting knights, always ready with the water, snacks, tea and biscuits. FatBum seemed to have arrogated to himself the role of the adjudicator, seated majestically at the head of the table, occasionally deigning to speak or raising a magisterial hand to guide the discussion and lower the temperatures.

'Banks do not give better deals to old customers. They always give the best to the new "*murgas*". The old ones have nowhere to go and so the banks presume they are stuck with them. That's when they raise the rate. Try as a new customer and you'll always get a better rate.'

'That depends on your power of negotiation and who you go to.'

'The best thing to do is move to a new bank at a better rate.'

'Really, you seem to know a lot. Please do let us know what happens to the prepayment penalty then? There is an existing agreement you know.'

'Calculate and see for yourself. Why do you need another person to tell you this? What is lost in the prepayment penalty is offset by the gain in the lower rate over the tenure of the loan.'

'Very good. Of course, and what happens when the new bank raises the rate one year into the loan? By then you have become old customers of the new bank too. What do you do then? Make another prepayment penalty and move to another bank?'

'Of course not. You negotiate at the start of the relationship for a rate that always matches the lowest the bank is offering at any point of time.'

'Why wait for a second bank then? Why not do that negotiation right now? Isn't that what I have been saying from the beginning?'

'Because the negotiation with this bank is already done. There is a paper that has been signed on both the sides. Any deviation from that will attract penalties. You, as a banker, should know that much at least.'

The battle raged back and forth…sometimes for a change of bank, sometimes for sticking to the same bank, sometimes, Abhijeet would make a point and then lean back, looking around expectantly as if awaiting applause, and sometimes, the sister's nephew's brother-in-law would score a hit and then issue forth a whinnying laugh to accompany it. Forever the wallflower in matters like these, I was more or less a silent and non-contributive observer. After more than an hour of this bitter crossfire, FatBum called time and summed it up for us.

Every bank is out to screw you, as is every developer and every agent. So, basically, everyone. They will continue to screw you until you scream, and scream you must, loud and long, and you must accompany that with the threat of taking your custom and chequebook elsewhere. That is the way, the recognized protocol for getting and continuing to get the 'best deal'. This is the advantage of having 'choices'. That is the beauty of this new economy—you are free, you are empowered and you can actually make choices. While FatBum was getting positively lyrical about the promise of the new age in India's dazzling future and the power of the empowered Indian consumer today, I was thinking, 'Wow! Finally we have a choice, a choice of whom to get screwed by—the new bank or continue with the old one.'

'You are just being unnecessarily cynical now. Why is everything looking so dark to you? These two guys have definitely been helpful to you and your landlord, Mr Khanna, he is right, isn't he? At least you have choices now. Twenty years earlier, perhaps you wouldn't get any loans at all; forget about negotiating on interest rates. He's probably remembering those times and speaking from that perspective.'

I have been telling Malati about the events of our dining table of a week ago. She has been telling me of the happenings behind the scenes at gagg.com. We are in a large airy room on the third floor of the Humanities section of the college. This has now been dedicated to the Arts Council and is honestly a great place to catch one's breath and generally catch up between classes. Though it is always full of students—some or the other project is nowadays always on—and Dr Pasricha has a table dedicated to himself here, it's still a happy place and Malati and I tend to spend our catch-up time here rather than in the staffroom.

'You should be happier, everything is going well. Your Wg Cdr Harjinder Singh is quite the hit on gagg.com. He's posted videos there explaining building by-laws and has a regular blog on "Rights and Responsibilities of Buyers". The old guy has found a new lease of life. He puts up photos of the construction update faster than the builder does on his own website. He and his wife are very much looking forward to shift; they want to be the first residents of Glenmont Greens. After all, they're having a terrible time living with their son and his family. You didn't know? It's common knowledge, the daughter-in-law wants them out, doesn't serve them dinner, doesn't give them hot water for their baths and what not.

'You do know the construction is up to the first floor now? You know that, right? Everything is moving along like clockwork. My nephew, of course, is very unhappy. When everything is warm and gooey, everyone loses interest—that's his contention. Because everything is so okay, it's boring. People will stop using the community. They have no grievance to share and thus, the objective of coming together is lost. He's planning to do something, start some thread or something, that will get people worked up and start fighting or talking or basically, just start using the site again.'

There's a group of students in yellow T-shirts practising a musical behind us. Much enthusiastic singing and dancing is happening. The music has a life of its own and it bounces from wall to wall as the yellow T-shirts whirl and twirl in perfect time. The room is large and brilliantly-lit by the afternoon sun. It is one of those nowadays-unheard of piercingly-clear Delhi winter days... Crisp, cold and cloudless. In such an environment, with the sparkling Malati Patel for company, it is indeed difficult to be unhappy, no matter whether you are getting screwed by the old bank or the new one. Maybe it's time to open up the ammunition pouches and uncork the water bottles for a refill.

'It's the home front, isn't it? That's why you are so morose. Did you find out whether it was your wife in Khan Market with Rocky? I mean, did she see us with her own eyes? Maybe you should have introduced us in the gagg.com meeting. Come on, snap out of it! She may be unhappy with you now, but as they say, this too shall pass.'

As if choreographed, the music and the dancing suddenly stop. The students gather together in a huddle for a murmured discussion. All at once, there is silence. I can almost hear an audible clang as the ammunition pouches and the water bottles snap shut in my mind.

'Malati, what are you doing this evening? Why don't we "witness some amazing scenes"? Your Mr Biswas needs a tutorial and I'll buy the drinks.'

Day 337

I T'S THE BEGINNING of a brand new year. Happy New Year to me and to all of us. Thank goodness some things do not change. The waiters at Aitbaar are as friendly as ever. The prices are still the same. Even the calendar on the wall is the same, it is still of last year. If anything, the only change here is in my status which has been elevated, thanks to Tubluda's impressive sally through the owner's range of Single Malts. I have been ushered into the 'premium' section where leatherette sofas replace the foam cushion on metal frame which is the standard decor. Warm and cozy from the heat of the electric radiator in the faux fireplace and gradually thawing from the inside where the three Blenders Prides I have had so far are blending pridefully, I am slowly pushing away from my consciousness the horrible 'Sirji' that has been haunting me ever since that awful property dealer repeated it ad nauseam to Roshni and me when we were in Gurgaon the week before last. 'Ji' is a Hindi honorific, an equivalent of the English 'Sir' or 'Mr' but, only in North India do we have the absurd practice of showing someone the fake respect of doubling the honorifics by conflating the Hindi and the English—each dignified and distinctive in its own right—into an inexplicable, double-barrelled hybrid 'Sirji'.

This Gurgaon trip was another one of our holy pilgrimages. This time it was undertaken in the lowering fog and mist which is the staple of Delhi winter mornings. Along with the clouds of fog that our Alto was, Titanic-like, coursing through, I was feeling frissons of excitement and hope once again. Imagine, me, the pretentiously intellectual and definitely very middle-class non-achiever, was finally going to get a flat in a Gurgaon condo. Maybe two years later—that's what gagg.com pessimistically has as the building schedule—but a Gurgaon condo apartment nevertheless. One has dreams when one is growing up but after growing up and coming to terms with one's place in life, those dreams normally get smothered under the cold blanket of reality. Of course, I too wrote all the statutory essays in middle school, 'My life's ambition', 'What I want to be when I grow up', 'Where I see myself twenty years later', and duly impressed the teachers with my noble sweeping ambitions of becoming an internationally renowned brain surgeon who comes back to India after a glittering career abroad to devote his life to bettering the lot of his less fortunate countrymen. 'A+', 'very different', 'good thoughts, well expressed', 'so nice to see something different from the usual fighter pilot ambition', 'this boy will do something in life'—those were the comments about me at the stage of life when I was confident of out-tubluing Tubluda. He stopped at dentist, I would be the doctor. He remained American, I would become Indian again. If I were a stock, that's when I should have been sold because that was the highest point. Unfortunately, I did not have the marks to pursue science beyond the secondary school. Unfortunately, there was nothing for an introverted arts graduate to do in the India of that time except for a post-graduation. Unfortunately, the interview board at the UPSC examination for the Civil Services turned me down. Fortunately, I secured a teaching job immediately. Unfortunately, I did not have either the drive or the aptitude to go beyond the college where I got my first job. Given the fact that the height of my ambition as a working adult was to make my position 'permanent and tenured' and not remain on an 'ad-hoc' or 'leave vacancy', Glenmont Greens was actually far and beyond my modest dreams after reality and age had reset the dream button of my life. So, there I was, happy and getting happier peering through the fog and keeping a fixed distance behind the blinking lights of the truck in front, en route the flat that would soon be mine.

'You know, maybe things will work out after all. That Abhijeet guy, your loan agent fellow, was saying that even without a fixed salary, I could probably get a loan as a woman entrepreneur. I mean my fashion consultancy and other things can easily be shown as an entrepreneurial venture and banks have a certain quota or something that they have to fill for women empowerment. Even the banks will want to give me a loan. I just need to get all the documentation right. That way, the extra money that we have to pay for this delay in construction will be easy to pay up. I mean, we won't really feel the pinch. What do you think?'

Replying in words was totally unnecessary. I just took my left hand off the gear shift knob on which it was resting and laid it over Roshni's hands in her lap. For the first time, we drove down to Glenmont Greens practically holding hands. In silence and in sharing, we were building our dream together. That is a memory, no matter what happens, I will forever cherish. That is a place to restock the ammunition and fill the water bottles to the brim.

'Cold water. No ice. One more please…and chilli chicken dry.'

All this liquor is reminding me of the two things that I was deliberately as well as desperately not thinking about when we were driving down to Gurgaon, that is, what happened with

Malati and me when we went out on that fateful day after college and the photos of Rocky on Roshni's phone.

Gurgaon was as Gurgaon is—manicured islands of affluence afloat a desolate sea of urban planning anarchy. The wintry fog was hiding the worst of the incomplete buildings and the forever under-construction roads. In fact, the whole atmosphere, with the chill and the fluffy fog, was rather dreamy. Glenmont Greens, like a seedling pushing its head through the topsoil and blindly seeking the sun, was rising out of the mists with its first floor complete and the roofing of the second floor going on. Draped in an overcoat with a shawl wrapped around his ears, the aged security guard listened to our proud claims of ownership of an 'eleventh-floor unit' and with a broad smile, flung open the gates insisting that we climb the stairs to the first floor and see for ourselves what our unit would look like, only that ours would be ten stories higher. 'The views would be much better' was his only comment, and 'Just don't fall off or jump off or I'll lose my job' his only warning.

'Look Roshni, I can put my study table here, so it'll get the winter sun.'

'This balcony has space enough for me to grow my flowers. Maybe I can even put in a planter box unit here.'

'And look at this! This kitchen is larger than I thought it would be. Maybe I can teach you some cooking too, eh Embee!'

'The sitting-room sofa set will go against this wall. We'll get it from this Internet site I've been following for the last six months; they have these amazing designs. And the curtains will come from that brocade and handloom place in Panipat that Aparna keeps talking about. Oh! Embee, it'll be lovely, very different from our wedding night *barsati*, huh? Imagine, we'll grow old here, sipping tea side by side on this balcony.'

As yet, it's just a floor plan come alive in concrete and brick.

There are no external walls, the fog is drifting in and out of the bare shell of the building and here are we, Roshni and I, zipped up to our scarf-trailing necks in fleece-lined jackets with woolen caps on our heads, holding gloved hands and imagining our warm and cozy home, breathing it to life in our minds. This is our living, breathing heart. This is where we will nurture the rest of our lives together. This is where we will set up our home, circle the wagons, put out the picket fences. It is ours, this hearth is our castle. This is the permanent address that all government documents keep asking for.

Had there been music, I am sure we would have danced our way from the unfinished naked steel-railing balcony to the gritty cement floor of the sitting room, only to find ourselves face-to-face with a stout, red-jacketed man framed in the doorless doorway.

'Mr Bhatia and Mrs Bhatia, I hope. Myself Tandon,' said this interrupter of our dreams, bearing towards us with his right hand outstretched for a handshake. After his 'hopes' were dashed—trust the optimistic Punjabi to replace 'presume' or 'suppose' with 'hope' in an English sentence—he adjusted to the fact that we were not the Bhatias he was expecting. Helping his 'adjustment' was the saving grace that we were, indeed, owners of a property here.

'Doomed, Sirji, doomed,' he said while rubbing his hands together as if he was enjoying himself; actually he was just warming his hands because later I noticed he was stamping his feet as well.

'Sirji, you should have done a little more research, na? Did you not come here in the monsoons? Then, how is it that you don't know what the problem is Sirji?'

When Roshni frostily informed him that this scattershot technique of his was not helping enlighten us, he suggested that we go for a ride with him in his Ford Endeavour, '4X4 sirji, fully automatic, top of the line and for madamji I have hot coffee in a thermos jar also.'

'Sirji, look around. Just see. This is in a down area. See, how down it is. This used to be a lake sirji, a *jheel*. Ask any villager and he will tell you. You can look at the old survey maps too; they show it as a listed waterbody. Even now, whenever it rains, all the water collects here. That is why I was asking you about the monsoon, *na*? They call it the run-off water. Why run-off, I do not know Sirji. After all, it does not run off *na*, it just stays here. You saw in the monsoon, *na*? The water stays here.'

Roshni and I remember too well how the water just 'stays here'. After all, this was the site of Roshni's infamous 'welcome to the swimming pool' address. However, I am still mystified as to what that has to do with us and, at my side, I can feel Roshni becoming stiller, as if she has a premonition of the 'doom' that is coming.

'Bribes sirji, bribes. Whole oceans of bribes were paid sirji. Seven future generations of today's politicians will bathe in these oceans sirji. That's how these few developers got the permission to dump soil and fill in these areas and changed the land-use clause to "develop" these lands. And please notice sirji, only these few developers—yours included—have "developments" in this stretch. This waterbody has been filled in sirji, homes, offices and shops have been sold on a lakebed and an ocean of bribes.'

Roshni has gone absolutely still and I am struggling with the zippers on the jacket pocket to get to my cigarettes.

'But don't worry sirji; God is Great. What goes around comes around. One environmental group had been after this issue for years. Water Watchers, they are called. You know wwatchers.org. They are very famous sirji. On TV also. Their thing is something about groundwater table becoming lower;

these geographical terms are so confusing *na*? Just think for yourself sirji, how can water have a table? Anyway, water table is becoming lower because of no recharge happening due to development here. Now, this group, you know, Water Watchers people, has finally been granted an injunction by the High Court in Chandigarh. Just last week sirji. All construction in this area has been stayed by the Court Order sirji. The water is safe sirji!'

Tandon's driver is driving the top-of-the-line Endeavour while Tandon is sitting next to him in the front seat. He turns around enthusiastically and beams at us—his ashen-faced passengers. Everything about this man is enthusiastic. He seems to be full of a vitality that he wants to communicate to all around him. It cannot be that he does not know the import of his news to us; after all, the first thing he confirmed was that we were property owners here and only a blind fool would have missed the chemistry between the first-time home-owners that Roshni and I are. And he is certainly neither blind nor foolish, yet, he is still so happy and enthusiastic as if he was the radiologist who confirmed to Roshni that she is pregnant with twins.

'Have faith sirji. Have faith in me. *Main hoon na.* I am here. Your flat can be traded sirji. That's why I was meeting Mr Bhatia. He has the same problem sirji. Even he and Mrs Bhatia have a flat here. Same thing, same problem. But I have a solution sirji. I can trade your flat. I have buyers who don't know about this thing yet and for the same price I can get you a flat in the Whispering Willows development. It is in Sector 48, sirji. There are no *jheel* or waterbody issues there sirji. Everything is dry and water-tight. Full registry and legal papers sirji. Only a slightly smaller flat, but a better deal sirji, a much better deal. No issues, at all. No issues sirji. No issues.'

'What? What are you saying? What is he saying, Embee?'

For the first time, Roshni has spoken. She turns to me and

the expression on her face literally breaks my heart. This is not only my house that I was congratulating myself upon achieving a short while ago. While I was being so full of myself about 'achieving' what I did not even dream of, could I not stop for a moment to even think what all this could mean for Roshni? Of how much human capital she has invested in this too? All I have seen over the past six months has been Rocky. With all sort of meanings construed, perhaps, only by me. How could I have been so blind? How could I not see what this means for Roshni?

'What do you mean, Mr Tandon? Do you mean that we sell this flat now? Before we even live in it? Before we even see what it is like? And move to what, what did you say, Whispering Willows, whatever that is. How can you say that, Mr Tandon?'

'I like this sirji! That's the pleasure of dealing with professional people like yourself sirji. You are all so smart, you understand things like this sirji. Like this!'

With this, he snaps his fingers together and continues, 'Sirji, the time to act is now. Tomorrow will be too late. With Mr Bhatia, I was going to close the deal right now. That's why I told the notary at the Court to be on standby. You see tomorrow this news will become public and then nobody will want to buy anything in these developments. And without the trade happening here, the Whispering Willows deal cannot happen, you know, sirji. But of course you know that sirji. All you professional peoples are so smart, you know and understand everything even before I say it.

'Here you are sirji. Your parking lot is here. The developer is very smart sirji, very smart. He purposely built this parking lot on the highest level. Even when you come here in the monsoon sirji, you can get into your car without getting your feet wet. That is psychology sirji, "Psychology" with a capital S!'

Tandon insisted on getting off and escorting a shell-, or maybe Tandon-shocked couple to their car. After getting us safely belted-in, and as we were about to depart, he delivered his parting shot,

'Sirji, yesterday a long-haired young fellow had come here with a movie camera. He said he knew you. Your name just clicked sirji, it just clicked. That fellow does something with the Internet, social marketing and all. He took an interview with me Sirji…with me! I had a copy of the High Court notice and he took my views. I told him sirji, I told him as a responsible real estate consultant who is familiar with the ground reality, I told him the real truth. However, he has given me a document sirji. We both signed one copy each. Nothing goes on-air or on the Internet till Saturday afternoon which means you have two more days to do the deal. Two more days sirji. You know everything. You are all too smart. You will always do the right thing. Have a great day sirji. You too, madamji.'

Day 337

*I*T'S STILL THE same day. It's still a Happy New Year. I am still drinking. All my chickens are coming home to roost. Be it chilli chicken or shredded or diced—it's all the same with Blenders Pride. Gagg.com has done it for me and for the hundreds of us who signed on. What have I done? How could I have created this Frankenstein's monster? This baby-faced long-haired monster, this nephew of Malati's, how could he do this to us? Is this the future we are heading towards? Intelligence with no connection to morality? Competence without conscience? The achievement of an objective with no thought of context or consequence?

'But uncle, the idea was to make this group active, to get people talking. I mean there has to be a "grievance" for a site like "Grievances Against Glenmont Greens", isn't it? That's why I put that video up. People have to have grievances. The whole idea is to get the community active and to get eyeballs uncle. This game is all about getting eyeballs.'

You got that Sonny. Not only eyeballs, you got us all by the balls. Us and hundreds of people like us who invested their life's savings. You got all that with that one video on gagg.com. It already has 325,000 views and climbing. The video of Tandon, cut so slickly, with the copies of the judgement and the site during the monsoons. Where did you get those stills I wonder? Not from my phone, well, at least, I hope not from my phone.

The commentary is the real killer. It talks all about the long-term sustainability of the next generation urban metropolis Gurgaon and how we ignore the warnings of today at our own peril.

'How can we presume to redesign Mother Nature's designs,' that was a gem, boy, a real sparkler. Indeed, how can we design a skyscraper on a lake? You should be happy now my long-haired digital sirji. You must be over the moon. There is so much of traffic on the site. It is an active community. There are lots of eyeballs, huge grievances. Only now, it does not matter how active the community is because the project is definitely doomed. No one is buying or selling anything there. No building is happening either. This time, this is not a clash between three Haryanvi brothers, no no, this time it is the government—with the entire force of the public opinion of an ecologically-conscious nation dedicated to saving its waterbodies to recharge its dwindling water table—that has mandated the stopping of the construction. Such is the power of social media. And, it all happened so fast! Yes, the court order was going to happen in any case but the developer would have found a way around it and greased some more palms to ensure that the flats do get built. That court order, like hundreds before it, would be overturned and accorded a silent burial. The march of progress would not stop for one dried-up pond. Perhaps, we would all have had to pay a little more. But now, with 325,000 people and more knowing about this, accompanied by some very intense media pressure about this "sensitive issue", we are all sure that we are all, like Tandon said, "Doomed sirji. Doomed".'

The air force has a tradition I am told. Whenever there is a fatal crash, all the flight-mates of the departed air warrior gather round in the bar at the mess and order a round in his memory. That is the military way of remembering the valiant.

'One more Blenders Pride please. And this time make it

large. Really large sirjeee. And don't disturb me, I am reading the newspaper.'

Wg Cdr (Rtd) Harjinder Singh and his wife, Dilpreet Singh, took their lives in a suicide pact three days ago after the developer announced an indefinite stay on the construction of his project, Glenmont Greens, in Gurgaon. Our reporters have found out that this retired Air Force officer and his wife were staying with friends when they took this extreme step. Earlier, they were staying at their son's flat in Dwarka but had shifted out after their son and his family came back from America. A handwritten note recovered from the site only talks about their eagerness to finally move into a place they could call their own. Sources claim that a PIL may be filed against the developer for breach of promise. One of the deceased was also the Secretary of the Flat Owners Group (FOG) of Glenmont Greens.

Day 337

THIS IS AMAZING. It's still the same day. I come back from the bathroom—all this water with all these whiskies you know—and it's still the same day! Very obstinate, this day. Stubborn. Like a mule. Just does not change.

Afghani chicken? What is this Afghani chicken? When did I ask for this? Did I ask for this? Or is it just another one of my chickens coming home to roost? This one must be Malati's. Same creamy complexion, same firm texture, same springiness of the flesh.

Where's the whisky sirji? Of course I asked for it. I am always asking for it. Ask Malati.

And, so we went out. Yes, we did. Before the world came crashing down on Roshni and me, before our house on the lakebed was revealed for all to see as a house of cards, we went out. Oh yes, straight from the staffroom to Palazzo, a little piece of Italy in South Delhi. I went with the signorina for the Vino and the Antipasto, yes, I did. Hoping for the dolce, I was. Ordered and drank a Grande Rosso, yes, we did, while messing around with the olives and the pepperoni. Allora! What an outing!

And we talked and we talked and we talked.

'I am more than happy being a friend to you.'

'Of course, I am genuinely interested. Why do you think

I spend all this time with you?'

'I know. I understand. I didn't know that your Wing Commander had such problems with his son and daughter-in-law. No wonder he was taking the lead in ensuring Glenmont Greens comes up the soonest. Of course, different people have different motivations, but I guess he felt he was at the end of his race.'

'I find this whole journey very interesting. In my own small way, I see myself also as contributing to your home.'

'Hey! Even I enjoy your company. You're a very interesting guy and don't let anyone else tell you otherwise.'

'Another glass of wine? Sure. It's certainly cold enough. Maybe it'll warm me up a little, eh!'

'Oh! I'm very flattered! Thank you very much indeed. Although what you see through these woolens and jackets is really beyond me. But, thank you kind sir. Thank you indeed.'

'I don't think so. No. No. We've had this discussion earlier too, haven't we?'

'Oh Mr B! Like I said earlier, I am a married woman. Anyway, why we can't we just be friends?'

'Look I have no hang-ups about any of this. I made that clear to you in Khan Market, didn't I? I mean even my husband knows. I've never had hang-ups ever. It's you who seem to be having hang-ups.'

'I told you I'm in a stable relationship. Even you seem to be very much in love with your wife. So what's up with you now then?'

'What is this? Some middle-aged man thing is it? Suddenly feeling your oats?'

'Take it easy. Take it easy.'

'Hints?! I dropped hints? What's with you, mister? Just because I told you a few facts about my life, you think I dropped hints? Jeez! You're so narrow-minded!'

'Get a life, you. Get real. We are all adults and let's behave like adults. Grow up! You want to be friends, that's fine, otherwise, you drink the rest of that wine alone buddy.'

'I don't want to make a scene in a restaurant but really, I am so turned off by your thinking. I really don't know whether we can be friends. You've turned out to be like all of those "typical" Indian men. And hints?! How dare you say I dropped hints? Who do you think you are? Go look in a mirror mister! Bloody small-town, small-minded nobody! Go and build your pokey little flat and live out your pokey little life. Dropping hints indeed. First time a good-looking woman is being nice to you and you think she is "dropping hints". Express just a little interest in his dreary little life for one minute and he wants to fuck you the next. Fuck off man!'

Awesome. Awesome. This Afghani chicken is just awesome. I'm an awesome fuck-up. My Bengali fish-curry-and-rice digestive system is not used to such good Afghani chicken. It's so good that I think I am going to puke.

Day 358

'BETA, MAYBE YOU should have taken that Tandon's offer. At least you could have discussed it with me, *na*? I could have found out from my local contacts about that Whispering Willows thing. You should discuss things more you know. Keeping everything inside just builds up the pressure.'

The Punjabi answer to most problems—and indeed, it is a very good answer—is food. Roshni and I have been called downstairs to discuss our house of glass and Mrs Khanna has cooked up a perfect storm. By the way, that's what we've started calling it now—the Glass House—because it's so transparent and everyone seems to know everything about it. And also, because all its illusions of security are so shatteringly fragile and yet how completely we seem imprisoned by it.

Maaki daal, *aaloo baingan*, *sarson da* saag, *methi matar*, three types of roti and naan, pakodas, papad, achaar, lassi, generous dollops of white butter—everything that you could think of from an authentic vegetarian Punjabi spread is all there. For the past half an hour, we have been dutifully gorging on the good stuff. The best thing about my problems, no matter how serious they are, is that they never adversely affect my appetite, plus of course, the food is truly outstanding.

The French windows of the sitting room are open. We are at the table which is by the far-end of the room—the dining section of the drawing/dining room—and the winter sun is pouring into the Khanna home. It is a spectacular winter's day after weeks of miserable cold, fog and grey polluted skies. The ever-present background rumble of traffic is much lower right now. Delhi had been battened down for the Republic Day Parade rehearsal and because of all the advisories issued by the police, there was comparatively very little traffic on the roads these past two days. The city seemed to be catching its breath, enjoying a much-needed respite from the daily marathon of the millions of vehicles on its roads. The Khanna garden is in its full winter bloom and its centrepiece is Rocky... Rocky in a black, sleeveless thermal vest and a matching pair of shorts. Rocky resplendent on the lawn. Rocky getting his Vitamin D. Adonis is in his own show-window. All is well with the world.

'Khanna saab, excuse me for two minutes please. I'll just go up and get my cigarettes. I seem to have left them in my jacket pocket and that's upstairs. I'll just come.'

Masterfully done. This will be the third time since we went downstairs that I've managed to come upstairs again. Each time the excuse is as different as it is creative. First, I need to find and get the file with the Builder Buyer Agreement (after all, is the developer going to return our money or not?).Then, I drop some chutney on my shirt and I have to go up again to change it (ah, clumsy me!) and now of course, I've forgotten my cigarettes. Absolutely masterful.

It is but a moment's job to enter the bedroom, open the wardrobe door, only one door is sufficient, reach into it, part the row of hanging shirts and jackets and have my hand settle unerringly on the neck of the Vodka bottle I have started stowing there. Quickly extract, twirl the cap open, raise, tilt, one swallow, exhale, one more swallow, replace the bottle's cap, opposite twirl and reinsert bottle. Twenty-four seconds from start to finish.

It's like a Seal Team Six Operation. The military would be proud. Now, the thing to do is to light-up quickly. Smell-wise, tobacco trumps alcohol. Always. But never chance it, talk less and always keep your mouth away from the listener. There you go. I am obviously a quick learner. Even though this kind of surreptitious drinking is new to me, I am startlingly good at it. No one's rumbled me yet and it serves to sort of mellow down the world. It takes the sharp edges off. Now I can go back and we can solve the problem of this bloody house.

'Fantastic food, Mrs Khanna, just fantastic. Sorry to have got up like that. Now we can have the oranges and the cigarettes outside on the lawn.'

See, that's what clear and decisive leadership is all about. Clear instructions with no options, yet, delivered as a request. In minutes, we are on the sun-drenched lawn, resting our newly fattened bums on FatBum's expensive garden chairs. There is a shaft of darkness though, in the vodka-fuelled and Mrs Khanna-fed sunlight of my mood. I notice an unspoken communication, a quick gesture between Roshni and Rocky, and Mr Muscles disappears inside the house, leaving the lawn to us. There is something almost peremptory about Roshni's gesture; it is as if she is dismissing Rocky, but why am I reminded of Malati? However, this is not the time to get derailed by these inconsequentialities, well, I hope, they are inconsequentialities. We should be concentrating on the main agenda of our business—us losing the home even before we've got it.

'So, Khanna saab, what do you think should be our way forward? I mean, you have helped us so much earlier and have been a part of this almost from the very first day. If you were in our shoes, what would you do?'

FatBum is looking strangely at me. Head aslant, eyes slitted, hands tucked into the pockets of his front-button cardigan, he is regarding me with great interest. Suddenly, he sniffs and gets up. As if to stimulate his own thoughts, he starts walking around us and talking at the same time.

'In your place, well, I don't know. Maybe I would have taken a knife to the developer. Just joking, just joking, don't think I am serious please. Just that, this situation will make anyone desperate. But you see, not just anyone, in this case, everyone will soon become desperate. This is something that will impact and therefore interest everyone, whether an investor or an end-user. I think that'll be the way to get him. If both investors and end-users come together along with public opinion then I am sure we can get him. And get him good.'

FatBum has circled around to where I am sitting. Once again, he is looking strangely at me. What is he up to? Good heavens, is he actually bending and sniffing me?! Has he figured out that I've been drinking? Is he trying to smell me out? How subtle can one get? Of course, I immediately turn the other way and light another cigarette. Why should I tell him, or even let him know, whether or not I have been drinking? It's my business isn't it? It is certainly not his.

'I don't know, I am not interested in taking revenge. My problem is not so much with the developer. I wonder if we can really blame him. He is just doing what everyone does. This whole place is built on robbery and creating value unfairly. Isn't this whole city, in fact, why only this city, everything in this economy built on doing something—what they call "creating value"—at somebody or something's expense? Earlier it was at the expense of the farmers, today it is at the expense of the environment, tomorrow it will be at the expense of something else. Why act so extra moral about it? Why should we be out to "get him"? We just want our home and he is our partner to get it more smoothly than we could ever have. What do you think, Embee? Could we have negotiated all these laws, regulations, permits, designs and all this by ourselves? Can you see yourself doing all the plumbing, electrical, materials, walls, doors, windows and God knows what else by yourself, Embee? Actually isn't the developer just doing for us what we cannot do by ourselves? So, why "get him"? Why can't we try and find a solution with him on this?'

All of Roshni's hopes, frustrations, dreams and disappointments are pouring out on the lengthening shadows of the lawn. I am sure FatBum has no answers. I certainly have none. I don't think anybody has. Mrs Khanna too has joined us on the lawn with a tray of hot, sweet, milky tea and the Punjabi *mathris*—a spiced flour cracker or the 'snack' with the tea—plus of course, her nuggets of homespun philosophies.

'*Beta, sab thik ho jayega*. It'll all work out. Don't worry so much, it's always the darkest before dawn. Put your faith in God. It's all His wish.'

'You know, Bungali saab. She is right. It will all work out. It has to work out. This problem seems very big right now, but actually it is not. There are just too many people and far too many big names involved. But, we must remember that so many scams have come and gone. What has happened? Nothing! This developer is not a milk-drinking infant, you know. He has been in this game for far too long now and there are far too many people in his pocket for this to not get sorted out. Just give it some time. Let this media storm blow over. What's it called? That film on the computer...ah yes, "viral". So what? After a viral infection, people get better, *na*? They recover and become fit and fine. Same thing will happen. Same thing. Don't worry. Stay as our guests a little while longer. No problem. Think of this as your own home only, *na*? We can always do some adjustment about the rent, that is a small thing, and it will be between us. But do not take too much tension my dear. Tension makes a person do silly things sometimes, you know, give into stupid desires, seek support in useless weaknesses.'

It's like being in a battlefield…actually, how would I know? Have I ever been in a battlefield? Okay, at least, it is how I imagine a soldier at the front line during sustained contact with the enemy would feel like. I am being buffeted around by swirling winds in a maelstrom of thoughts. So many emotions are assaulting me together. Roshni's evident anguish is a stab to the heart. Mr and Mrs Khanna's still-rustic warmth and goodness is a balm to the soul. There are still people like this in this city. There is a wealth of profound wisdom in their assurances of 'everything will get better', a numinous insight in the simplicity of Khanna's 'after a viral infection, people get better, *na*?' My own tensions at the events of the previous few weeks are slowly being soothed. I am feeling a sense of serenity and peace that I have not felt for a long time. Sinking a little lower into the garden chair, I marvel anew at the greenness of the lawn and the colours of the flowers that have bloomed all along its edges. I bet Roshni could name each one of them.

'You know Roshni, Mr and Mrs Khanna are right. Something has to work out. There are just too many people involved. And not to sound cynical, but the kind of people involved are not the slum-dweller types whose homes are demolished overnight and everyone forgets about them by the morning of the day after, after a lot of shouting on prime time news about their rights. The kind of people involved here are not going to let anyone forget about them in a hurry. Perhaps gagg.com will truly come into its own now and finally serve a higher purpose.

Of course, you are right too. Nobody is out to 'get' the developer. That would definitely be counterproductive. You are right, we need to work with him and find some solution with him. We don't know the first thing about house-building and without him, we would not know our way around this maze at all. But what is this? What is he wearing? Why? Why's he walking like this? What's got into him?'

'Relax Embee. That's a part of my upcoming spring collection. I thought it would be nice to see it in this late afternoon light.'

It's an incredible sight. Rocky has rejoined us and is strutting around the edges of the lawn. He is wearing an intricately folded and beautifully patterned dhoti—or maybe, it is a baggy, just below-the-knee length pajama—that leaves his flexing and striated calves bare for all to view. His upper body has a sleeveless fabric mandarin-collared shirt that is tied with strings that are loose around his chest and become progressively tighter as they come down to the waist. To me, it looks like it is shoe-laced, however, there is no denying that the overall effect is rather nice. As a matter of fact, Rocky looks majestic. Wildly incongruous in the context perhaps, but majestic nonetheless.

'That's right. Just turn to the left, will you? I want to see the colours of the fabric against the light. Yes, that's enough. OK, come here, that's enough. Thanks. Just tell masterji to take out two stitches from the back and put in the paisley pattern I showed you, remember, the thin stripe? Yes? That stripe from the armpit to the waist on both the sides. Cool? Thanks.'

'I think your son will become a model after all. Needs to work a little more on his ramp walk, but I think he has a good modelling career awaiting him.'

'Roshni Beti, thank you so much. Really. It is a godsend for us that you are here. Our boy now has a direction. I have never seen him working so hard on anything. He is really trying to become something and he is really grateful to you. I can see that look in his eyes whenever we talk of you. And, don't you forget, even more than our son, you have our gratitude too.'

While Mrs Khanna is getting sentimental about the change that Roshni has brought about in Rocky's life, my mind is racing ahead. Could I have been mistaken about Rocky and Roshni? Could I now hope that the closeness between them has just been professional and that Roshni has merely been using him as a model? Or is this just another one of my fond imaginings and that there is a truth that is much murkier? What is this 'look' that FatBum's wife sees in her son's eyes? Is it the same look I see, or can the same look say different things to different people?

'Professor saab, once again, you are thinking too much. You are worrying too much. And man to man, while our wives are talking, you are drinking too much. Why? I ask you, why? What is the reason? Arre, these things happen while building a house. This is not a real problem, your house will happen. This is nothing much—so many people have more serious problems. And all these problems are only a matter of time. Like most problems, just give it some time. And what is that thing Rocky keeps saying about the gym...ah yes, no pain, no gain. So, some pain will be there. What to do? You will have the pleasure of being your own landlord in your own lifetime. Now, don't worry so much about it. And till then, we are there, *na*? So, what is the worry?'

My vodka-induced high has worn off. The afternoon has meandered into a shadowless, grey evening. Soon, it will be dark with the sudden duskless onset of the night that took the British visitors to the subcontinent by such surprise. The cloying hospitality of the Khannas and the fashion sideshow of my wife with their son playing alongside is proving to be too much for me. Gesturing to Roshni that I am going for a walk, I excuse myself, thank the Khannas profusely for their hospitality, their advice, their support and most of all, for their sheer niceness, and set off on one of my rambles. One more plus on the strangeness scorecard my dear Roshni, this man likes to walk—aimlessly and purposelessly perhaps, with no objective and for no good reason—but he likes to walk.

The rivers of traffic in this city now no longer have banks. Every last footpath has been swallowed up by tar and run over by the rush of motors. Plus, they are no longer seasonal or diurnal, they are perennial and forever in spate with the cars of the day being replaced by the trucks of the night. Just like fast-flowing rivers always have a fine mist of water droplets permanently suspended over them to create the rainbows that are the poets' and the photographers' delight, these rivers too have a visible halo of auto exhaust, unburnt fuel and kicked-up dust particles around them. Just like the roaring of a river's waters can be heard from afar, the roar of the traffic and the atonal symphonies of honking that emotionally-disturbed drivers set up can be heard from almost every home in this city, at any time of the day or night. Primitive man may have been driven to religion and the invention of easily comprehensible or identifiable anthropomorphic Gods by the stillness of the night and the silence of wide-open spaces, we have no such fears. We are far more evolved. What need do we have of anthropomorphism? We are in no doubt of the fact that we are in the middle of a thriving, bustling, modern megapolis; what need we be plagued by such primitive fears and primitive inventions? Whatever our different religions might be, we all now worship the common and faceless Gods of wealth, competition, greed and violence because they provide us the security and the sustenance that the anthropomorphic Gods of the previous tens of millennia did for humans earlier. Why, I wonder, in spite of such sophistication of thought and transposition of belief should we be still anchored to the idea of a home for security? Should we not have transcended this base need a long time ago? Especially, considering the cities we live in?

I am no longer rambling…at least, not physically. I have reached the Ring Road and I cannot, literally, cross it. Nowadays, there are no pedestrian crossings on this highway that rings Delhi. Every intersection has metastasized into gigantic and convoluted ribbons of tarmac that sometimes go up, sometimes down, sometimes to the left and sometimes to the right. What they all share in common is a complete disregard for any sort of pedestrian convenience. Continuous, bumper-to-bumper traffic thunders down the road. Behind me are the privileged enclaves of South Delhi. Ahead and across the road are the government flats, markets and older colonies that once marked the perimeter—the Southern Extension—of the city, around which the road was laid like a ring. Like the yogis and the mendicants of yore who meditated on the banks of rushing mountain rivers, I too perch myself on the railing at the side of the road and gaze down with a sick fascination at the raging torrent below. The sages breathed in the fresh mountain air, while I inhale auto exhaust fumes. The sages had ample reserves of bhang, ganja and charas, the byproducts of the cannabis plant, for their moments of narcotic epiphany, I have my 'quarter' of Magic Moments vodka which has quite magically found its way into my jacket pocket as I passed the English Wine and Beer Shop enroute here. Perhaps, this will be my Bodhi Tree, this will be the place where I will achieve the supreme understanding at the heart of all things, the place where I will attain urban nirvana.

Day 379

$\mathcal{P}$ROFESSOR SAAB, YOU are such a wonderful teacher. Your students absolutely worship you and you have, quite frankly, been an inspiration to many other teachers too. Do you know that your method of electronic notes is being followed by colleagues from other departments too? You know, your dictating notes into your cell phone and later having them digitized and circulated among the students? That is such a creative method, absolutely wonderful, really, full marks on that. And the work that you have done with your Arts Council idea? That is also outstanding, really brilliant. Sad that Mrs Patel had to leave and immigrate to Europe to join her husband, but now you have Dr Pasricha practically full-time on this to help. You don't seem to realize it, but each of your initiatives has brought great credit to the college and we are really proud of you. You think of different things so easily and all your thoughts make the lives of the students easier and certainly much richer. You have been a great asset, professor, a true gem, a sparkling diamond of our college.

'That is why I am so distressed to see you like this nowadays. What has happened to you? Tell me how we can be of assistance and we will be standing tall for you. Definitely. We are always there by your side and will mobilize all that we can to help you tide over whatever it is that you are going through. But

Professor, we cannot have what has been happening for the past six weeks, can we now? After all, we are an academic institution, aren't we? And we just cannot afford to have our faculty drinking vodka during the day in the staffroom, can we? You tell me that? You leave us with no options, sir. No options at all. You tell me, what would you do were you in my position? Tell me, sir? Please tell me.'

Mahendra Lal Sharma is a good man. A great man, even. A committed educationist. Unlike most of us in the staffroom, an academic career did not come to him while he was waiting for life to happen. He chose it and he chose it for the passion that he bears towards the profession and the undimmed hope that he continues to have that every man can and does make a difference. His is the passion and the strength of mind that gives up a tenured position at the University of British Columbia, turns its back on a 16-acre hobby farm in Vancouver and the easiest of possible lives and comes back to India because 'we all make a difference'. 'I am a Ballimaran Boy. I was studying in Hindu College when rabbits were being snared at Bhikaji Cama Place, when we counted three motor vehicles in 90 minutes at Dhaula Kuan and only monkeys played and peacocks danced where there is now Jawaharlal Nehru Stadium. So, of course, I had to come back to Delhi. All of us should have something to give back to the city, don't you think?' This quintessentially good man is the principal of our college and he had this conversation with me some twenty days ago. A conversation that I am sure was far more uncomfortable and painful for him than it was for me. A conversation after which I have been placed on leave—with all the support of the college, of course, to sort out whatever issues I might have—to do some thinking. Of course, more than thinking, drinking is happening. I am, for the record, on an 'academic sabbatical'. Had I been a student, I guess the term would have been 'suspended'.

Ratna Pishi visited us a fortnight ago. One of the many things I seem to have underestimated is Roshni's grasp over the Bengali language. After we finished our dinner and saw Pishi down to her taxi, cleaned up the kitchen, locked up the doors, dutifully double checking the latch on the door going up to the terrace, and stood shoulder-to-shoulder on the tiny balcony attached to our bedroom—really the place for a single clothes rack—me, with a cigarette and she with a cup of green tea, Roshni revealed to me that her understanding of Bengali, even of the nuances of the language, is devastatingly accurate. Not only of the language, her understanding of moods and her insights into Ratna Pishi's psyche too was truly illuminating.

'I think this attempt to get the house from Tubluda was the last flicker of the candle's flame. Her life has changed so much ever since she started queening it over in this CR Park house, I think, she sort of convinced herself that this was rightfully hers to grab. Of course, that lawyer fellow—that scheming scum—egged her on. He must have thought he'll get himself a fat deal without too much effort. Ratna Pishi put everything she had into this throw of the dice and she lost it all.'

'How? Why do you say lost? After all, she is still staying there. What really has changed?'

'C'mon Embee, you did hear her, didn't you? More than hear, you should see her...really see her. Can't you see, she has lost her spirit, that special animation that she always had, that I-know-best attitude. Did she try to boss over you today? No, right? She didn't boss me too. She didn't even complain about the taste of the food or that her tea had too much sugar. Come on, six months ago, she would have made the tea herself just to show us how it's done. And her sari? Forget about starched, I don't think it was even ironed properly.'

'I see what you mean. But really, I don't want to assume anything, especially after what I told you of that old Subedar Major Mukhopadhyay's attitude to life. Maybe Ratna Pishi too is preparing to face the reverse swing bowling of her last overs, after all, even she knows she is no spring chicken anymore and this is her way of preparation?'

'I don't think so. I think your soldier boy is very different from our Pishi. This lady has just given up. She is physically giving up too, you can see that, can't you? I mean, choosing to go to a Briddhashram, an old age home in Kolkata? Who does that when you have a perfectly good house to live in? Perhaps Tubluda has made life really difficult for her here.'

'She didn't give you any details, did she? About why she is going and what exactly it is that Tubluda has done to her?'

'On second thoughts, somehow the impression I got is that this has nothing to do with Tubluda. He and his lawyers just ensured that all the paperwork was in place and it was legally clear that she was a tenant and has absolutely no claims on the property. No, she's got nothing against all that. It's just that she's lost all interest in living here now. Like I said, she staked everything on getting this for herself and now she's realized the futility of it.'

'You mean it's a "the grapes are sour" kind of thing?'

'Not at all. More like she's understood that the grapes were actually sour all along and she thought they were sweet. How beautifully was she reciting that Tagore poem *"Dui Bigha Jomi"* and how tellingly did she put herself into the ending –*"Sadhu hote chollam aaj, chor chilam bote"*, you know, "I'm trying to be a Sadhu today, but truly thief is what I was".'

'You understood all that? I thought you were just, you know, humouring her. Well, I didn't know you had read Tagore's poetry and all and that you could understand her changing the last line. Well, anyway, how was I to know?'

That was when Roshni gave me one of her 'Roshni looks' and announced bedtime. Since that day two weeks ago, I too have been trying to understand Ratna Pishi's meek surrender or as Roshni conversely said it the next morning, her 'victory of understanding'. But I must confess, I have not been able to. The fact, however, is that Ratna Pishi has left Tubluda's house in Chittaranjan Park. In fact, she has left the city of Delhi altogether. She is now a permanent resident of an old age home in Kolkata with the dues being paid by a sort of pension fund that Tubluda had set up for her in order to meet the monthly household expenses when she had first moved to CR Park. I still don't understand her move, in spite of my many sessions at the 'rivers of contemplation'.

I'm having another one of those sessions today, those quiet, calm, meditative sessions, trying to cultivate stillness in a storm. A session that gets better as the night gets darker. I have staked my claim on the riverside, confident in the knowledge that the rushing traffic will never abate. I am secure with the experience of many nights like this that the pell-mell confusions outside will only multiply...that I will rise far above all this and my Magic Moments will take me to the still-heart of the mystery. It has rained a bit today. The winter is not giving up without a fight. Delhi's bipolar weather is on full peacock display. While the heaters have not yet been packed up and dispatched into storage, some days are hot enough for people to take the covers off the air conditioners and give them a test run. After a few sunny days, winter has descended once again to reclaim its hold—sort of clearing its throat—with a drizzle in the evening of a dreary overcast day. I too have been adventurous and instead of my usual meditation spot on the side of the Ring Road, I have headed southward to the Outer Ring Road. This is another one of Delhi's imaginatively-named roads, laid in one more ring around the original ring in a vain attempt to contain the city after it frothed and foamed wildly across the first ring. Here too I am not disappointed—cars, buses and trucks roar along in a steady and uninterrupted cascade, while two-wheelers, like darting minnows flashing silver in a river, flit in and out of this steady rumble. Illicit and mobile cigarette stalls—which open in the evenings, fold up late at nights and trundle away at the first sight of an unfamiliar and therefore ungreased and unfriendly policeman—are my meditation halts. For the investment of a single cigarette, I can retire into the shadows and contemplate life as it rushes by and analyse my attempts to put down roots in this raging torrent. All this is, of course, alternately illuminated and sedated by the glimpses of nirvana that furtive sips of Magic Moments allow.

I had made our pilgrimage today. Only, I made it solo. I had gone to Glenmont Greens, our homestead, but I had gone alone, hoping against hope that perhaps something was happening there. I did not even think of driving, instead, I took the metro and an autorickshaw from the last metro station. The first thing I noticed was that the signboard had cracked and broken, the flex, that had been ripped in half, was hanging down and flapping in the breeze. The morning dew had condensed and concentrated all the ambient pollution and there were runnels of black and coarse grey in diseased zebra stripes down the tattered sign. Trying to relive a precious moment of the past, I had walked up to the first floor. This time, there was no security guard to either check or encourage me. I walked across the entire floor again and retraced the steps I had taken with Roshni. Yes, think positive. Everybody says it will all work out. If it were not so, then Gurgaon is entirely an illusion. Everything around is false, done only with smoke and mirrors, simply because everything around has been built on the same foundations, on promises as fragile as my glass house, on plans as chaotic, on schemes as villainous, by people as unscrupulous, approved by politicians and bureaucrats as self-serving. If everything else worked out, then why won't this? Why should my house be the one to be made an example of? Why should all morality, scruples and concerns for the environment be focused only on Glenmont Greens? While I was thinking these thoughts, I had walked out to the balcony where Roshni was visualizing the placement of her pots and planters the last time we were here. The happiness that we had felt there was still lingering as if our chemistry had imbued the place with something special. This is certainly one of those forward bases of the subedar major, a place to fill those water bottles to the brim. As if mirroring what I was thinking, I noticed that a green shoot had taken obstinate root in the bare cement which comprised the balcony's floor. Just where the unfinished cement floor, hanging out in the air, met with the raw steel rods that would one day form the balcony's railings, this green shoot was capped with a single purple flower. Fluttering in the breeze, this was certainly a Magic Moment for me.

'Smiling? Of course I am smiling. We should all be smiling. One Classic Mild please. Here you are, exact change.'

'Arre saab, you can afford to smile. You will smoke your cigarette and go back to your happy home and warm bed. What about us? Where are our happy homes and warm beds? Money makes you smile sir. We don't have your money. How will we have your smiles?'

No, no, no my friend. Today is not one of those days when you will engage me in philosophical disputations. Today is not the day for conversations with itinerant cigarette sellers. No, my friend, sorry, but this is my time alone. I am jealous of it and I will guard it fiercely. This is the time to be spent at the rivers' side, the time for Magic Moments, the time for me, the time for my memories, the time to work on the pursuit of happiness. Sorry again, but I have no time for you. I only have time for a long and satisfying pull at the Classic Mild and, of course, for my Magic Moments which, by the way, is artfully concealed in a sleek runner's sipper—a beautifully streamlined bottle that comes complete with a spill-proof cap. To complete the illusion, Artful Me is also dressed in an Adidas track-suit with a similarly branded cap on my head. I have a brother who is a big-shot in the United States, that's America for you, OK? That's where I get all this from. OK? Back to meditation…OK. Back to gazing at the river. Back to beautiful moments at Glenmont Greens.

For a moment, I thought I should pluck the flower and take it back to Roshni. Then, better sense prevailed. Plucking it would destroy everything we were hoping for that is, a proof of life in our happy home. Isn't that the term kidnappers are used to being asked for? Something they need to produce? A proof of life? Of course, our dream is not dead. There is that elusive proof of life. This is a magic moment. So, I took a picture on my ever-present cell phone. It is the time for another Magic Moment. By the way, I have learnt how to use the earphones perfectly now. There's a little button on the control midway on the wire between the phone and ears which you can use to stop, replay, record everything; basically you can control the whole thing with your thumb.

Floating on a cloud of happiness, I turned back from the balcony. Yes, everything will work out. This is too big to be torpedoed by a few shrieking environmentalists. Some way will be found…for sure. Here I am, in the sitting room. This is where Roshni wants the sofa from that website and the curtains from that place in Panipat. Well, she shall jolly well have both. Even if 'jolly well' sounds like Tubluda. This doorway leads into the kitchen. This is where she will teach me cooking. I remember her clearly, 'And look at this! This kitchen is larger than I thought it would be. Maybe I can teach you some cooking too, eh Embee!' The kitchen is looking, if anything, better than it looked the previous time we were here. There is a double-bowl stainless steel sink installed. Was it there the last time? Certainly worth a closer look. I must tell Roshni about it. This definitely calls for another Magic Moment.

Large. Well-formed. Perfectly-coiled. With a smattering of dried liquid brownness. Not steaming still, but fresh enough for the flies on them to be so intent on their task that they were unmoved by my one look. There is one in each bowl. Human turds.

Certainly another Magic Moment. This time, in Initial Caps.

Yet another cigarette stall.

The Ring Road roars, rampages and rushes around with the revving of restless, reckless retards. What had Malati called it? Alliteration. That's right, alliteration. Something made popular in English by someone named Gerard Manley Hopkins. That's what Malati had taught me. I miss her too. I miss my English lessons. My study of A House for Mr. Biswas remains incomplete. Maybe my glass house will remain incomplete too. However, that's absolutely fine with me... The new me. I am now enjoying the situation. I am an enjoyer and not a sufferer. It's as if I have been granted a reprieve, as if I am one of the very lucky, very few to escape with life from a particularly malevolent, almost-hundred-per cent-fatality record kind of disease. I am not getting sucked into situations, rather I am staring at them from the outside. I am laughing at them, as I was doing inwardly when Malati was tying herself into knots trying to explain to me that her precipitate departure had nothing to do with our al fresco fiasco at Palazzo.

'You see Mr B, it's a great opportunity for Purshottam. His business becomes global in one stroke. And for that, he has to be based in Brussels.'

'Of course, I am not playing the role of the "Bhartiya Nari", the traditional Indian wife who'll always say that my place is at his side, etc. It's just that it's so good for me too. I've always wanted to explore the influence of the continent on Victorian British Literature and now I can do a PhD on the subject.'

'No hard feelings Mr B. No hard feelings at all. I am sure we can share a bottle of wine again sometime. We should remain friends, after all, we did exchange so much.'

'Oh! Come on, this is not a business deal, so, no handshake nonsense. Come, come, give me a hug. Give Princess Patel a goodbye hug. Of course, I know what they call me in the staffroom.'

Purshottam. Imagine that. This is a Sanskrit Sandhi. Even the Germans have it. It means the joining of two words to form a third where the meaning of the third word is actually the meaning of the two words without a conjunction. Purshottam is *Purusho mein Uttam*, without the *mein* in between. The ultimate or best amongst men. So, Malati was married to the Ultimate Man, or the Bestman Patel. But shouldn't his name be Yuvraj? After all, Yuvraj means Prince. Prince Patel for Princess Patel. I am sure that could be argued in a court of law... See here Your Lordship, we have Prince Patel, the perfect consort for Princess Patel!

All this rambling is making my throat dry. Another cigarette is needed. And Your Lordship shall provide me with one. Lordship? O cigarette seller, My Lordship!

By the way, who made you Lordship? I agree to the Lord

bit, but why ship? I ask you, why ship? You're such a little guy, you should be called Lordboat. Give me a cigarette, Lordboat. You are a good-looking little guy though. Bet you're a big one with the ladies. Let's change your name then to LordBeau. C'mon Lordbeau, give me a cigarette.

C'mon Lordbeau! One cigarette. Lordbeau!

ROSHNI

15 June 2017. New Delhi.

It's been more than four months now since that awful day. I was just not ready for anything like this, never had the experience you see, but then, that's Embee and what he calls, his 'strangeness quotient', always pushing you into situations that you are unprepared for.

Tubluda was a big help. He came down from the US immediately and just took over all the administrative nitty-gritty. He spent a lot of his own money too and every time I would ask, he'd just say, 'He's my kid brother you know.'

An even bigger shock was Devika showing up a month later with a whole ream of typescript in her canvas sling bag. She just handed it wordlessly over to me with tears in her eyes and left sooner than she appeared. It was then that I entered the secret world of my husband.

Once again, I am all over the place. If Embee was standing over my shoulder, this is the point at which he would say, 'The point, Roshni, get to the point and stay with it.'

OK. So, here's the point. The facts are as follows:

On the night of 8 February, my husband met with an accident on the Outer Ring Road at the shopping centre opposite IIT gate.

The accident was not fatal, however, he has still not

regained consciousness. Doctors are hopeful though.

There were several eyewitnesses and some participants. There was an argument, a scuffle during which Embee was pushed, lost his balance on the slippery, rain-slicked surface and fell on to the road. A car speeding down the road could not brake or swerve in time and knocked him down. He travelled some fifteen feet. He has a fractured hip, and both the shin and the thigh bone of the right leg are broken. He also has severe internal and head injuries.

The primary witness is the cigarette seller/vendor. His eyewitness account is that Embee was slurring his words and swaying when he reached him asking for a cigarette. According to him, Embee was abusive and referred to him using a particularly objectionable Hindi slang term—not to put too fine a point on it—he called him a dick. Apparently, his slurring of 'LordBeau' sounded really offensive to him. Two other customers present on the spot took strong exception to this and remonstrated with Embee. However, this remonstrance was in the typical Delhi fashion. Since they were physically bigger and Embee was obviously not in complete control of himself, they slapped him around and knocked him down. Trying to get away, he slipped, skidded and literally bounced on to the road where he got hit by the car. The two men who knocked him down have disappeared.

I was summoned immediately. The same cigarette seller scrolled down the cell phone call list and rang my number as the last dialled. Mr Khanna, Rocky and myself took him immediately to the Emergency Room at the hospital, where because of the Khannas, we got immediate attention.

While fumbling with his phone to dial my number, the cigarette seller inadvertently emailed all the audio files in it to the contact ID that was the default ID set for audio files.

Embee used to dictate all his lecture notes as well as anything else that he though could be helpful to the students into his cell phone. That audio file would then be e-mailed to Devika, a typist who did this freelance, to type-up as a print copy for Embee and its soft copies—not the audio files—would be sent to all the students. This is an innovation of which he was justly proud and, since imitation is the sincerest compliment, an innovation that was speedily copied by other colleagues.

Devika thus received all of Embee's personal ramblings over the previous year. Obviously, she typed them out or started typing them as a standard procedure. As she put it, once she started typing, she just could not stop. And after waiting for more than a month, she gathered up the courage to hand over the typescript to me because she thought I would be the best person to know what to do with this.

She was wrong. I am not the best person. I still don't know whether I am doing the right thing by sharing Embee's ramblings like this. Since I did not know what to do, I called Mr ML Sharma, Mr and Mrs Khanna, Tubluda, Dr Dhingra (he is Embee's attending physician) and invited them over for coffee. I asked them what they thought I should do. Obviously, this is a shock for all of us. It seems like such an invasion of Embee's privacy and my husband is a very private man.

We spent days discussing this. Our combined opinion was that while it is very painful for us to pry so deeply into his personal space, the average reader would not know Embee and therefore it would not be so personal. We all felt that this is not our story alone—while we might not be doing this in a professional way like Embee tried with gagg.com—this is a story that needs to be told because this is something that is common to hundreds of thousands, maybe millions, of *home-builders across our country. Perhaps Embee's thoughts could be of some use to many more people than us alone. I imagine it like Embee speaking to us from the hospital bed. Plus, of course, there was the fact that bits and pieces of this had started popping up on the Internet—perhaps somebody else too had got hold of the recordings—and we thought it was best for Embee to set the record straight in his own voice and with his own words.*

We decided not to edit at all. Let the personal references remain as they were. Perhaps we will issue a second edition after this with Embee's edits, after he wakes up and sees how we've bared his thoughts to the public. I keep telling him that in the hospital. I've even shown him a copy of the book. Dr Dhingra says it's a good thing to do, perhaps we'll get a reaction this way. The only person we've fictionalized and edited a bit is Malati, but saying anything more would be saying too much, so we'll close that particular topic now.

At an individual level, it was deeply painful and at the same time frankly exhilarating to read Embee's thoughts. It was as if Embee was speaking, which I guess he was. Of course, I knew of his drinking, but I did not think it had reached such levels. It had happened once before too, some five years ago, but since then, Embee kept it strictly under control. I am absolutely sure that he will get it under control again and that this is just a passing phase. And for the record, Rocky is a fashion model and nothing more. In fact, everyone in our group affectionately calls him 'numbskull Rocky' or 'Rock Solid Rocky'. I admit freely that I cried copiously and unashamedly when I read about Embee's feelings about how far we've drifted. I no longer have any interest in Glenmont Greens. When he wakes up, we will leave this city. This place no longer has any space for us and there is no longer any space for this place in our hearts.

I hope you enjoyed reading my husband's thoughts. Please do not make the mistakes we have. Please make your own. Do come and visit us at the hospital if you can. But make it quick, because Embee is going to recover fast and after that we are off.

I'll sign off here with a mail from Tubluda which he'd given me permission to include in case the publisher agreed to publish this.

From: dr2blue@gmail.com
To: Roshnibee@yahoo.com

28 May 2017

Dear Roshni,

Hope you are bearing up well and keeping the faith. Never forget the power of positive thinking. Remember, it's always the darkest before dawn. Things will get better but before they get better, they will get worse. They always do. No doubt, Bublu would be sniggering at this and saying to himself— 'Vintage Tubluda, there he goes, talking in clichés again.'

I am glad you have chosen to publish. Yes, by all means go right ahead. I know that I have not been painted in a kindly light, but it is what it is. We all do what we think right when we think it is right. Hindsight or another's point of view, both of which are always so illuminating, are unfortunately not available when we are in the middle of the action.

You will perhaps be happy to know that I have put the CR Park house on the market. I will be selling it to the first buyer I get. Strangely, I have not got any yet. However, I am not going to be taking that money out of India. You keep being formal with me, but please understand we are family. That money, first the interest from it and subsequently, if required, the principal too, is dedicated to Bublu and you. Use it well. All these medical expenses can be killing. Believe me, I know, how do you think I got rich?

OK, now, this is what I want your readers to know—the one thing that Bublu has missed out on. We discussed this often and often mused about it. Our parents used to tell of the legends of the Gods and would tell often of the race between Ganesh and Karthik. The one in which they needed to circle the world thrice to be the first to eat the fruit that Shiva and Parvati, their parents, were offering. Karthik took off on his peacock and whizzed around the world in double-quick time while Ganesh just ambled around his parents thrice. That's what we were, and I think, still are—me, the winner of the world 'Bishwajeet' and Bublu, the winner of hearts and minds 'Monojit'.

Warm Regards,
Tubluda
(Dr Bishwajeet Bhaduri)

www.ingramcontent.com/pod-product-compliance
Lightning Source LLC
Chambersburg PA
CBHW030329020726
47493CB00004B/1207